Nate Beck nosedived

The last few inches meant safety and freedom. But he was too late.

He jerked his head and arms back before they were pinned between the descending garage door and the pavement, and then crouched against the metal barrier. His eyes widened and flashed in fear as he searched for an escape route.

"Stand up, Mr. Beck! Slowly!" the cold voice of the assassin shouted as the man walked toward the trapped merc.

Beck noticed the blood on the sleeve of the killer's jacket as the man methodically attached a long thin silencer to the barrel of his gun.

The assassin raised the weapon and aimed.

The shot echoed throughout the almost empty garage. A brief sunburst of blood and bone exploded into the darkness of the underground parking lot.

The assassin seemed to smile, and then slumped to the floor.

Liam O'Toole had pulled his trigger first.

**Now available in the exciting series
from Gold Eagle Books**

SOBs
by Jack Hild

SOBs
SOLDIERS OF BARRABAS

DEATH DEAL

JACK HILD

A GOLD EAGLE BOOK FROM
WORLDWIDE

TORONTO · NEW YORK · LONDON · PARIS
AMSTERDAM · STOCKHOLM · HAMBURG
ATHENS · MILAN · TOKYO · SYDNEY

First edition November 1986

ISBN 0-373-61615-5

Special thanks and acknowledgment to
Robin Hardy for his contributions to this work.

Printed in Canada

1

It was meant to be a nice little coup d'état, quick and easy, neat and clean, but it didn't turn out that way.

Walker Jessup paused to gasp for breath as he stepped out of the Banco Nacional and into the Plaza Murillo, the central square of downtown La Paz. His cream-colored summer suit displayed big dark patches where his perspiration had soaked through. The overweight Texan tugged a handkerchief from his breast pocket to mop the sweat from his face. It was futile; the handkerchief was as limp and damp as he was.

La Paz, the capital of the South American country of Bolivia, was situated in the Andes, more than four thousand meters above sea level. At that altitude the air was very thin, and the sun burned through the cool morning like a brand through paper. It took years of living there for a man to acclimatize. Even a healthy man would be out of breath.

Walker Jessup weighed in at around three hundred and fifty pounds, walking testimony to a dedicated passion for gourmet food. He regretted his flabby condition almost every day, and never more than now. He stuffed the handkerchief back into his pocket. On the benches around the square, old men slumbered, or slowly rose to move into the shadows cast by the Spanish-style colonial buildings. Carrying little satchels for shining shoes, Indian children, dressed in rags, their faces dirty, ran toward the Western tourists outside the hotel on the other side of the plaza. An old woman spotted Jessup. She walked toward him with her eyes closed, extending a tattered felt hat and begging for a few coins.

The hotel was across the plaza, a few hundred yards away. He set his eyes on it and lumbered forward.

On his left was the presidential palace, the home and office of the chief Bolivian executive—a weak and ineffectual man whose days were numbered if Jessup didn't get to a telephone fast. Directly across the square, the tall columned portico of the National Congress stood in shadow.

To Jessup's right, next to the old cathedral, was the National Treasury. Under the previous regime it had been known as the Palace of Laughter. The basement of the elegant colonial building had housed the infamous torture chambers. Many had entered the great wrought-iron portals that led to the inner courtyard, but few had left alive. Jessup shuddered.

Soon the Palace of Laughter would be back in business if Walker Jessup's clients had their way. For the hundredth time that morning he cursed himself.

Walker Jessup had earned his nickname, "The Fixer," honestly—in a manner of speaking. After twenty-five years in the CIA, private enterprise had beckoned. He specialized in covert actions of interest to any government, agency, business or individual who had the bucks to pay for his international network of informers, bribe takers, and dealers in arms and influence.

The man who had visited him two weeks earlier in his New York office had been most persuasive about his honorable intentions when he had asked the Fixer to help arrange a coup d'état. Such affairs were common in Latin America, and normally the going price wasn't high. The current president of the small country wedged between Argentina and Chile was lukewarm toward the security interests of the United States, and definitely troublesome as far as Bolivia's debt repayment to Western banks was concerned.

This time, Walker Jessup had to admit he had done it for the money. The lure of 1.6 million dollars was damn near impossible to resist. If he didn't do it, someone else would. Quickly the Fixer had gone to work.

He had greased the palms of bureaucrats and government officials in half a dozen countries to ensure that they would take pains to look the other way. Friends in high places in Washington had promised to acquiesce in exchange for future favors. He had arranged for the delivery of millions of dollars' worth of arms. And when the junta took power, it would be through the Fixer's good graces that they would receive instant diplomatic recognition in Western Europe, and substantial lines of credit to American and Japanese banks.

It had all gone perfectly smoothly—until he had arrived in La Paz two days earlier to put the finishing touches to the setup.

From the moment he had met the other conspirators he had sensed something; an instinct from deep within him had warned him he was playing with hellfire. It had troubled him briefly, but soon it was buried under the accumulated details of the job. The night before, though, he had had the dream. Nightmare was more accurate. He had woken up shouting, drenched in sweat, haunted by the image of an army of jackbooted soldiers marching over him.

Back home in Texas they said it was the kind of dream that made a man go blood simple.

He never did get back to sleep. He had spent the next few hours combing through his notes, looking for a clue to the source of his anxiety.

At 8:00 a.m. he had rushed to a final meeting with the Bolivian conspirators. Suddenly, as he was talking to one of the leaders of the junta, it was as if someone had snapped on the light in a slide projector and had adjusted the focus. He had recognized the man.

Age and plastic surgery had changed the face. But the Fixer had known, sure as lead kills, that he had been in the presence of a kind of evil no one messed with, not even for more than a million lovely little U.S. bucks. He had slipped away from the meeting and had deposited his notes and briefing material in a safety deposit box at the Banco Nacional. It had been a precautionary measure. The number of the box was on file in his New York office. Now he had to get to a telephone and get help.

Jessup heaved and panted, his trachea scraped raw, his lungs squeezing what little oxygen they could from the air. He stopped momentarily at the bottom of the short flight of stairs that led up to the grand entrance of his hotel and mopped his forehead once again. He blinked away the salty sweat that stung his eyes.

Half a dozen dirty-faced, barefoot Indian children rushed toward him like a swarm of flies, pulling at his sweat-soiled suit and waving their little shoeshine bags. He plowed through them and wedged himself into the revolving door.

Inside the hotel lobby, the conditioned air slapped him in the face like a cold towel.

"¡Señor...!" the clerk called from the desk. "There is a message from—"

Wordlessly Jessup put out his hand to shut the man up. He headed straight for the bank of telephones on the wall behind the elevators and squeezed into the narrow old-fashioned wooden booth. He dialed the operator and waited. It took forever. There was no word for urgency in Bolivia.

"Please, please." He closed his eyes and prayed. His fingers drummed on the little shelf where the phone book lay. "Pleeease," he begged to whatever god in heaven was responsible for the phone system.

"*¿Sí, señor?*" The high-pitched nasal voices of telephone operators were the same everywhere, no matter what the language. Jessup gave her the number in New York and rattled off the digits on his credit card.

"One moment, *por favor*."

Again he waited, shuddering on the verge of panic. The receiver, pressed tightly against his ear, filled with static and the tiny distant voices of other conversations on crossed wires. Half a world away, he heard the New York telephone ringing. Once. Twice. It stopped. Someone picked it up.

"Answering service."

Jessup almost collapsed.

He had forgotten about the time zone. It was one o'clock in the afternoon in New York. His secretary was out to lunch. As usual. The wry thought momentarily steadied him.

The operator came back on the line. "Do you wish to continue the call, *señor*?"

"Yes!"

"You may go ahead."

"It's Jessup. Walker Jessup."

"I'm sorry, sir," the New York voice answered. "Mr. Jessup is not in, and his office is closed until 2:00 p.m. Would you like to leave a message?"

"This *is* Jessup!" he shouted, catching his breath in angry frustration. "Never mind. I'll leave a message for my secretary. Tell him to contact Barrabas. Nile Barrabas. The number's in my Rolodex. It's ur—" a shadow suddenly fell across the phone booth, and Jessup turned "—gent," he finished slowly. Six men in civilian clothes surrounded the booth, blocking him from the view of the hotel desk and the tourists in the lobby. A short man in a trench coat slid the door open with his foot. He took the telephone receiver and replaced it in its cradle. With his other hand he raised a .357 Magnum.

"You were saying, *señor*," he said in a voice as thin as barbed wire. "Something about your friend Barrabas? We will take care of him. And you can keep talking."

The Hispanic arched his eyebrows and pushed the Magnum's long deadly barrel into Walker Jessup's open mouth. "To this."

2

In Geneva Nile Barrabas flipped through the documents quickly and looked up at the elderly white-haired man on the other side of the desk. There were several pages of dense, small-print legalese in several European languages.

"It's all Greek to me, Hermann," the former American army colonel sighed. "I trust your judgment. Where do I sign?"

"Never trust." Hermann Heinzmuller stated gruffly. The Swiss attorney pushed his chair back, stood up and walked to the other side of the desk. He pulled a chair up beside Barrabas and jabbed his finger at the top document as he sat down. "Not even me. My commission on these investments I make for you is at least ten percent higher than what a legitimate broker would charge, and you say nothing."

Barrabas smiled at the old man. Heinzmuller had been handling his finances through the Geneva office for years. "I have no complaints, Hermann.

From what you've been telling me, the return on my money is substantially higher, too.''

Heinzmuller winked and proffered a silver fountain pen. Barrabas shuffled through the documents, scribbling his signature on the lines his attorney pointed to.

"So you're a rich man, Nile. You don't need to work. So retire. Find a nice woman, settle down. Start a family, and you won't even think about where this money came from."

Barrabas laughed. "Like you, Hermann? You're at least thirty years older than I am and you're still wheeling and dealing."

"Nile, I deal in nice things. Safe things. Stocks, bonds, securities. What do you deal in? Nasty things. Things that don't like you. It's a miracle you're still alive and sitting in front of me. In thirty years, for you, who knows? Tomorrow, for you, who knows? I don't like to wrap up estates, and I don't want to lose your business."

For a moment Nile Barrabas looked thoughtfully at Hermann Heinzmuller. The Swiss attorney dealt with money. Barrabas dealt in death. Never had the two men spoken openly of the mercenary leader's line of work.

For many years after he had left the army as one of the Vietnam War's most decorated veterans, he'd hacked around in grimy little countries fighting bushfires for whatever side came up with the most cash. All that had changed a few years earlier when

Walker Jessup had hired him to put together a covert-action team to secretly free-lance for the U.S. government.

His team was made up of a highstrung, competitive collection of borderline lunatics. But the SOBs—the Soldiers of Barrabas—had already made him proud on more than a dozen successful missions. And would again.

Since the growth of terrorism and competition between the two superpowers after World War II and Korea, all the rules had changed. The world was being ripped in two by extremists of the right and left. Sometimes it seemed like no one was going to survive.

Barrabas was convinced that as long as the SOBs were around to kick ass, the planet had a fighting chance.

"Hermann, you know that English expression about the dogs of war? Shakespeare wrote that, didn't he?"

Heinzmuller raised his eyebrows, slightly surprised. "You rarely reveal that you're such a literate man, Nile. Yes, Shakespeare." He raised his arm in a flourish. "'Cry "Havoc" and let slip the dogs of war.' *Julius Caesar*, act three. I love that play."

The colonel smiled at the old man's erudition and scribbled his John Hancock at the bottom of the final document.

"Well, Hermann, it used to be the dogs of war. Now it's just dog eat dog—except my teeth are longer and sharper than the rest. Otherwise I wouldn't be so rich.'' He handed the pen back to the old man. ''Right?''

Heinzmuller laughed and slapped his knee. Pointing his finger at Barrabas, he said, ''*Ja, ja*. That you are, Nile. You trust me. I should trust only you as much.''

The portly attorney and the tall white-haired colonel stood simultaneously. Heinzmuller glanced at the thick gold watch gleaming on his wrist. A large diamond ring on his little finger caught the light. The attorney loved luxury and had spent his life working hard for it. ''Closing time. Where do you go now? Can I give you a lift to your hotel?''

''Nope. To the airport.''

''The airport? You don't stay to enjoy the sights of Geneva, this beautiful city where, how is it you Americans say, the women are so willing?''

The mercenary leader smiled in spite of himself. He didn't want to offend the kindly old man, but Geneva was a banking town, and the night life was so dull it made a Florida retirement community seem like the Club Med. ''I want to fly on out of here.''

''And where to?''

Barrabas shrugged. ''Depends where the next plane goes, Hermann.''

Heinzmuller sighed again. ''I trust you. I respect everything you tell me. But I don't understand you.''

''It keeps life interesting. I'm between jobs and between girlfriends, so I've got time on my hands.''

"Then let's go."

Heinzmuller's office was located in an elegant stone building in the old section of Geneva, just off a central four-square-block area where Switzerland's famous banks huddled shoulder to shoulder. It was after five, and most of the city's office workers had departed for their homes in the outlying suburbs along the shores of Lake Geneva. Low gray clouds hovered overhead. The narrow street was wet from an afternoon of light winter rain. They got into the attorney's dark green Fiat Spider, which was parked at the curb of the worn cobblestone sidewalk.

"It's the only sports car that gives me room to wear my hat," Heinzmuller explained, pulling into the narrow deserted street. The little two-seater had a surprising amount of zip.

At the first corner he turned right onto the grand processional avenue that led through the heart of the ancient city. The heroes of Swiss history, cast in bronze and carved in stone, watched them silently as they proceeded across the wide stone bridge over the Rhône River.

"You like the nice things in life, Hermann," Barrabas commented, glancing in the rearview mirror on the passenger door. "I would have thought you'd be driving something a little more sophisticated."

"Rich people can't afford to be obvious these days." Heinzmuller winked and deliberately scratched his nose to display the egg-sized diamond in his ring. "The world is evil. Kidnappings! Murders! No one is safe. Not even an old Austrian Jew living in Switzerland. Now I wear a wristwatch of solid gold, but under the watchband are the numbers that the Nazis tattooed on my skin forty-five years ago at Bergen-Belsen."

Heinzmuller turned quickly through a neighborhood of dreary, decaying apartment houses. The streets led downhill toward the ramps to the autoroute on the northwestern perimeter of the city. The last rays of the evening sun filtered past the imposing snow-covered massif of Mont Blanc. In the distance, the cold waters of the mountain lake, which was famous for its startling blue color, shone like silver under the darkening clouds.

"Besides, this isn't an ordinary Spider."

"I'm glad, Hermann. Because a dark blue Peugeot has been following us ever since we left your office."

The elderly attorney's friendly chatter abruptly ceased. His knuckles visibly whitened as he tightened his grip on the steering wheel. Quickly he glanced at his rearview mirror. The Peugeot was almost half a kilometer behind them, keeping its distance in the quiet evening traffic.

After a moment of shocked silence, he asked meekly, "You're sure?"

"Not yet. Can you make some diversionary turns?"

"Diversionary? What is this?"

Barrabas glanced at his attorney long enough to see that the old man was extremely frightened. In the past few years most Europeans had seen enough terrorism to justify their fear.

"What have you got in this thing?"

"A special carburetor, *ja*? It gives me more speed."

Barrabas nodded. That also accounted for the extra pickup when they had left the curb.

"More than a hundred thousand francs I paid for it. And the backs of the seats are armored with aluminum plates two centimeters thick."

"Okay, that should stop a few bullets."

"Bullets! Nile, I did it for amusement, not to be serious. I'm only a poor Swiss attorney with no political connections!"

"Don't get excited, Hermann. First things first. Let's see if they're really tailing us. Then we'll decide what to do about it. Turn left here."

"But the airport is—"

"Hermann, just turn left. And speed up. Just a little."

The Swiss did as instructed, accelerating past the intersection and into the curve. The next traffic light was three blocks away, and it was green.

"Slow down," Barrabas told him.

The Spider slowed just as the Peugeot turned the corner and came into view. The distance between the two cars had decreased dramatically by the time the Peugeot braked.

Barrabas kept his eyes on the green light ahead. On the other side of the intersection, the street changed abruptly to one way—the wrong way. A sign with a slash through a large red circle warned traffic not to enter.

"You got a gun?"

"But they are illegal in Switzerl—"

"It's okay. I do." Barrabas reached inside his jacket and slipped his Browning HP from the concealed holster. It was a simple gun but extremely effective. The thirteen-round, double-staggered line box magazine was a useful feature.

"Now keep your speed down, Hermann. Nice and easy does it. Wait till the light turns red."

The light turned red.

"Go for it!"

Hermann Heinzmuller turned pale and looked at Barrabas. Herr Colonel wasn't kidding.

"Now, damn it!"

Hermann knew this was it. Not just for Barrabas. For the good fight. He gritted his teeth, gripped the wheel, steeled himself and floored it.

The little Spider shot into the intersection just as the traffic on either side started across the white lines. A cacophony of horns erupted from the cars as the drivers braked and turned to avoid collision. The headlights of the car facing them on the one-way street blinked madly as the driver tried to warn them of their mistake.

Hermann braked slightly and pulled the right wheels over the curb. He swerved around the oncoming car, lurched back into the road and accelerated.

The din of blaring car horns faded behind them, only to be following by screeching tires and the resounding crash of metal impacting against metal.

"Very good, Hermann." Barrabas smiled, turning around to look at the attorney. "They were definitely following us. But they didn't make it across the intersection."

Heinzmuller smiled nervously, flushed with pride. He quickly turned right at the next intersection into a narrow alley sandwiched between old brick warehouses. It led downhill to an esplanade along the bank of the Rhône.

"*Ja*, it's very exciting, just like an American movie. But why—"

Fifty meters ahead a black Renault drove into the street and squealed to a halt, blocking their entrance to the esplanade.

"Hermann," Barrabas said with a touch of whimsy. "We've only just begun."

IN NEW YORK CITY it was Liam O'Toole's big day. The phone rang at 9 a.m. on the dot; it was the call he'd been waiting a long time for. But the Irish-American tried to pretend it wasn't there for the first few rings. He moaned, buried his head in his pillow, squeezed his eyes against the gray morning light and the raucous Greenwich Village traffic and tried to go back to sleep.

But the caller was persistent. On the tenth ring O'Toole cursed, jumped out of bed, threw the pillow across the room and reached for the phone. As he stretched toward the bedside table, his leg struck flesh. Warm, soft flesh. A female of the species. Oh, no, he thought, what have I brought home this time?

He glanced quickly as he picked up the receiver. It was a brunette, with soft white skin and delicate features. Not bad, he thought. She clung to the sheets, blissfully unaware of the phone, the light, the traffic and the universe. Lucky girl.

"Hello," O'Toole rasped into the mouthpiece. He cleared his throat to add timbre. "Hello," he said again.

The man answered in a volley of words. He sounded very New York.

"Liam? Liam O'Toole? Ted here. Ted Merkin, from Crow Books. Lee, baby, how ya doin'? Ya sound great. Look even better. Listen, about *Maggot Picnic*. It's a great book, a great poetry collection. There's no question we're going to publish it. You're gonna be famous—just a matter of details. Got an agent? Doesn't matter, don't need one. We'll give you a great contract, the best. Whaddya say, Lee, baby?"

Suddenly Liam O'Toole was alert. His poetry was very dear to him, based as it was on his life as a seasoned warrior—first in Vietnam, at present as the second-in-command of the Soldiers of Barrabas.

War might be hell, but writing was purgatory. Liam O'Toole poured his heart and soul into his poetry. It took guts—raw, pure nerve—to confront the terror of the blank page each time he sat down to write. He was good, too. More than good. He was great. *Maggot Picnic* was more than just a personal statement—it was literature, in the cause of which he had endured more than his share of rejection, insult and humiliation. The low point had come when some punk rock group had turned his stuff into a video obscenity. But O'Toole knew that genius was rarely recognized in its time and had resigned himself to literary limbo.

Now this guy at Crow Books said he wanted to publish it. Just like that, out of the blue. For a few seconds O'Toole was convinced this was just more bullshit. They were stringing him along. Building him up so they could all laugh when he tumbled. But Crow Books was a giant in the publishing industry. Maybe this time it was all for real. Maybe this time.

"What did you say your name was?"

"Ted. Ted Merkin. Executive Consulting Senior Editor here at Crow. Have we got a deal, Lee, baby?"

"Maybe I should come in and see you."

"Great idea, wonderful. How 'bout two o'clock this afternoon." Merkin gave him the uptown Manhattan address. "It's a great book, Lee. Brilliant.

You're gonna be a big hit. Make you a million bucks. The new Rod McKuen.''

"I'll be there," O'Toole told him, hanging up. While he was on the phone the pretty brunette had moved across the bed and had circled her arms around his leg. She clung tightly, murmured in her sleep and wriggled between the sheets. It was starting to come back to him now. They'd met at the bowling alley on West Thirteenth Street. Liam O'Toole knew all the places where the lonely hearts hung out.

He fluttered with excitement. "That was the main course," he muttered, referring to the phone call as he slipped down into bed again. "And you, baby, are going to be dessert."

At ten to two that afternoon, O'Toole was whistling his way across the plaza that led to the office tower's main doors. The security guards inside gave him only a passing glance. He examined the directory. Sure enough, Crow Books had seven floors, from thirty-six to forty-two. Merkin had told him they were in the midst of moving. His office was now on sixteen.

O'Toole's anticipation grew as he rode the elevator and stepped out on sixteen. The recognition he was due was finally on its way, and he couldn't quite believe it. It had been a long, hard struggle, and he'd paid his dues. At one point he'd even paid a vanity press to print a thousand copies of his own book.

The elevator bonged delicately to announce its arrival on the sixteenth floor. He stepped into the corridor and saw the handwritten cardboard sign indicating Crow Books on the two doors opposite. He shrugged. Merkin had already apologized on the phone for the total chaos that the move was creating.

O'Toole opened the door and walked into a huge open office area the length of the building, with windows looking into the concrete canyon outside. The move obviously hadn't progressed very far. He faced thousands of square feet of wall-to-wall carpeting.

"Lee, baby! You're looking great, looking great." A slender man with a goatee emerged from a partitioned office at the far end. "Don't mind the mess. We're just getting settled. Come down here into my office."

Merkin's office bore a greater resemblance to what O'Toole had imagined the inside of the Crow Books empire would look like. Hundreds of new paperbacks were strewn in piles on the floor, and Merkin's desk was piled high with a disorganized tangle of papers. *Maggot Picnic*—the vanity press edition—lay front and center. Once again O'Toole felt a thrill of anticipation.

"Have a seat, Lee, baby," Merkin said, walking around the desk and sitting. He motioned to the metal stacking chair across from him. "Sorry about the disorganization."

"Liam," O'Toole said politely. "My name's Liam."

"Okay, Liam." Merkin's voice had changed tone slightly. He picked up the copy of *Maggot Picnic*, looked across at O'Toole and suddenly sneered. "You call this poetry? I call it crap."

Merkin threw the book into the corner of the room. His hands dropped below the desktop into his lap.

O'Toole felt the bottom drop out of his entire life. For a moment he didn't believe it was happening. Was this an elaborate hoax or something? They'd lured him all the way here just to make fun of him?

"You call this a joke?" Liam said slowly as he started to rise. "I'd say it was a pretty bad one."

Merkin's hands returned to the desktop. This time he held a Smith & Wesson M-39 in his right hand.

"You call this a gun?" he asked smoothly. "I call it time to die."

3

"Whooaaaa!" Lee Hatton shrieked as her skis slipped out from under her, tumbling her unceremoniously on her rear end in foot-deep powder snow. The tangle of skis, poles and limbs made her look like Bambi unsuccessfully taking his first steps.

Geoff Bishop swooped down the hillside, his skis parallel, and deftly turned his legs to one side. A small wave of snow fell across Lee as he came to a perfect stop.

"Hey, thanks a lot," she protested lightly, brushing the snow from her dark blue nylon ski pants.

"The hardest thing about skiing are the falls," the Canadian pilot said earnestly.

"Yeah. It's been almost ten years since I skied as a schoolgirl. No one told me I'd have to learn all over again."

She lifted her legs gingerly, trying to sort out the tangle. When she finally had her legs parallel, she pulled herself up the ski pole Bishop proffered.

Immediately her skis started slipping down the hill again. She teetered precariously, swinging her arms out like a tightrope walker.

"Whaa...heeelp!" she shouted, grabbing at Bishop.

He laughed and grabbed her around the waist.

"Remember. Angle the edges into the snow!"

Lee turned as best she could and angled into Bishop, pressing her face against his with a little smile.

"I did it on purpose, silly. Give me a kiss."

Geoff Bishop smiled. For a moment he forgot about skiing in Quebec's famous Laurentian Hills, north of Montreal. These were the moments he lived for, when he had Lee Hatton all to himself.

They had met as members of the Soldiers of Barrabas. Lee—Dr. Hatton, as she was known professionally—was the squad's medic, as well as an expert in acupuncture and the Filipino defensive art of Escrimo.

Bishop had been one of the Canadian air force's top pilots. Later he had flown jets commercially. Now he was the airman the SOBs depended on. The two of them were lovers in their off time. But only off time. When they were on assignment, it was strictly business and pass the bullets, please.

Despite their honest attempt to put aside their feelings for each other when they were on the job, their relationship was an open secret among the other mercs. Sometimes it caused problems—particularly with Alex Nanos. The Greek felt protective toward the only woman on the commando team. Or maybe jealous. Tensions between the two men were constant, and on occasion the situation became explosive.

It made Bishop feel as if he always had to watch his step. But not here in the Laurentians on a glorious winter day. The snow-covered hills spread to the edge of the purple horizon, with ski runs slithering like long white snakes between the brown winter forests. Overhead the sky was deep blue. Despite a temperature just below zero, the sun shone warmly on their faces. And Mother Nature had given them a foot of freshly fallen powder snow. Problems were a world away.

"Promise me one thing," Lee sighed after a moment.

"Anything," Bishop answered dreamily, mesmerized by the way her dark liquid eyes melted into his.

"That you'll never tell Nile or any of the others what a terrible skier I am," Hatton answered with a laugh, pushing herself forward and skiing down the hill. "Last one down's a—"

She got three meters before she promptly fell, landing in the same tangle she'd just extricated herself from.

Bishop laughed in spite of himself.

"Time for you to learn how to get up all by yourself," Bishop said as he skied to her side.

Lee pouted.

"Straighten your legs," he instructed. "That's right. Now dig your poles into the snow and use them to pull yourself...great," he concluded encouragingly as she pulled herself to her feet, feigning great weariness.

Once again Lee tipped, falling against Geoff and giving him a bear hug through his red-and-black ski suit. "Why don't we go down to the lodge and—"

He felt her stiffen slightly, even through the layers of clothing. "What's—"

"We're not alone anymore," she said.

Bishop turned his head to look uphill. A skier in a dark ski suit and wearing yellow goggles against the snow glare stood on the promontory above them. He seemed to be watching them. Almost immediately another skier appeared, stopping smoothly beside the first.

"Well, it couldn't last forever," Bishop said, referring to the absence of other people on the slopes all morning.

The first man was undoing the zipper that ran down the front of his ski suit. Lee pushed herself away from Bishop and pulled her ski poles out of the snow.

"Last one down—and this time I mean it—gets to..."

Bishop kept his eyes on the two skiers thirty meters uphill. The other one began to reach inside his ski suit, too. The first pulled out a submachine gun.

Bishop grabbed Lee's elbow. "Let's go," he said firmly.

The man aimed the SMG downhill.

Lee saw it, too. "Shit."

The glorious winter day was over.

Orange muzzle-flash and the sound of automatic weapon fire clouded the day. Bishop and Hatton pushed off, disappearing quickly over a rise and out of view. The autofire stopped, but both of the mercs knew that their attackers were right behind them.

"Hold your skis in!" Bishop ordered Hatton. He deliberately braked to stay behind her a few feet. It was a helluva way to learn, but she seemed to remember everything he'd told her that morning. Even as he watched though, her legs slipped inexorably farther apart.

"In!" he shouted harshly, knowing that as they accelerated on the downhill slope it would become more and more difficult for her to maintain control. He skied up beside her as she wavered, grabbing her elbow, lifting and holding tight.

She straightened.

"Come on, that's it! That's great!"

He could see her face, pale, frightened, but nevertheless determined.

The ski run forked. The main run went almost straight down, two kilometers or more to the lifts and chalet far below. It offered their attackers a long, clear view of their escape. In their colorful ski suits, they'd be like plastic ducks in a carnival shooting gallery. The run to the left was marked with a yellow sign, indicating advanced skiers only.

Bishop went for it, turning Lee gently by twisting her elbow.

The staccato chatter of autofire chilled them again. Bullets zinged over their heads like invisible metal wires. As they swung around a protective copse, the autofire stopped momentarily.

The run began with a slight upward incline. Then there was a small jump a meter high, dropping off to a steep slope that cut through the thickly forested hillside.

Lee tensed when she saw it.

"Relax, baby!" Bishop told her. "Lean into it and coil like a spring." He let go of her elbow.

Lee knew she'd done it before, years before as a teenager. It was just a matter of letting her body remember. Like a parachute jump. She imagined making a perfect landing in her mind's eye.

She went up the incline and left the earth, sailing two meters over the snow. The steep white hill came up fast. She felt her body wavering, steadied herself and drew her knees in slightly. Her skis touched, disappearing into the deep powder. Weight forward, she thought, leaning into the cushion of the slope.

Suddenly the run curved almost ninety degrees to the left. She sucked in her breath and shifted her weight. A bump, hidden by the layer of powder, jarred her, buckling her knee. She wavered, but was able to steady herself.

Then her left leg flew out from under her. She fell backward and sideways, while her body continued forward in a reckless tumble down the nightmare slope.

THE PARTY WAS JUST ENDING as the sun rose over the Sierra Madre of southern Mexico and splashed across the white hotels of Acapulco. In the Inferno Room of the Hotel Diablo, a number of deeply tanned men clung to the last threads of the night before, their soiled and wrinkled tuxedos evidence of deep commitment to their life-style. They wove their way wearily from bar to dance floor like zombies in a voodoo film.

Alex "the Greek" Nanos had taken up position, drink in hand, black tie askew, near the great portals that led to the grand staircase spiraling down to the elegant lobby. His room was on the twenty-second floor. He wanted to go there more than anywhere else, but only if the young woman who stood beside him came, too.

Her olive skin showed she was unmistakably Hispanic. Her soft, sensuous lips were bright red, and her black hair fell in thick, light curls down her bare shoulders. Perched over one ear was an elaborate corsage of pink orchids. She wore a low-cut, hip-hugging, floor-length silver lamé dress that made her look like she'd been shrink-wrapped and flavor-sealed.

Nanos was dying to unwrap her.

He'd already invested more than an hour in her. First he had told her all his jokes. She had found them amusing. Then he had talked about his athletic pursuits—scuba diving, parachuting, mountain climbing. She had been impressed.

Finally he had worked his way around to weight lifting. She had liked that a lot. His tight-fitting tuxedo did little to conceal his broad, well-built shoulders and thick biceps. He had offered to show her the real thing upstairs. Still she had demurred.

All the way to third base, and he couldn't get home.

"Shit," he muttered under his breath, quickly turning his back to the crowd.

A very tall dark-skinned man with a barrel chest approached from across the room. William Starfoot II was known to the SOBs as Billy Two. At six foot six the full-blooded Osage from Oklahoma stood almost two heads taller than the average Mexican in Acapulco. Even the oversized tuxedo barely fit him. He looked like a giant penguin, and about as comfortable as an Antarctic bird caught in the tropic zone.

He spotted the broad-shouldered, dark-haired Greek near the door and made his way over.

"Alex."

Nanos was still caught in earnest conversation with the lusciously smiling raven-haired South American beauty.

Billy Two tugged on Nanos's sleeve.

The Greek smiled in defeat and turned around.

"Billy, this is the millionth time tonight you've bugged me. And for the millionth time..." He leaned closer and whispered between his teeth. "Can't you see I'm busy. She was last year's Miss Uruguay."

Billy Two leaned around the Greek and stared blatantly at the woman, examining her up and down with a studied glare as if she were meat in a supermarket. "She looks like one of those foil-wrapped chickens they barbecue on spits at the super—"

"Billy," Nanos growled. "Scram. Vamoose. Get out of here."

Starfoot nodded. "That's what I've been saying all night. Let's get out of here. I got creepy feelings. And Hawk Spirit won't come to a place like this. I don't like it when he leaves me alone. It makes me feel—"

"Lonely."

"Vulnerable."

Nanos sighed in resignation. Billy Two was his best old buddy in the whole world, but ever since the Russian secret police had tortured him by injecting liquid sulfur into his veins the native Indian hadn't been right in the head. Hawk Spirit was supposedly his ancestral warrior guardian spirit. A psychiatrist might refer to it gently as an invisible friend. Or clinically as schizophrenia.

Admittedly Billy Two could do some pretty interesting tricks—claiming that Hawk Spirit was responsible. But there was definitely a limit to what Alex Nanos believed in, and right now the limit was defined by the neckline of the former Miss Uruguay's silver lamé evening gown.

Nanos leaned in close and put his hand on Billy Two's shoulder. "Look, old buddy. She's just about to drop for me. Go upstairs to the suite. Grab some shut-eye—in your own room. I'll be finished in a while. Then we'll do something. We'll go fishing or something."

"But Alex—"

"Hey, Billy. Let's get it straight. I got a need that just won't wait."

Reluctantly Starfoot left. Ten minutes later Nanos got to home base. Miss Uruguay agreed to let the Greek show off his muscles.

Once they were inside the luxury penthouse suite at the top of the Hotel Diablo, the formerly coy ex-Miss Uruguay became one hundred percent vixen.

Nanos slipped off his jacket.

"Maybe a little champagne," he said. The bottle in the ice bucket had been waiting all night for this.

"Oh, no, Aleek," she purred, clutching him fiercely and pressing her pelvis against his leg. Her hands slipped between the snaps of his shirt and worked their way across his chest.

Nanos gulped.

"I need you," she said breathlessly.

"I need you too, babe."

Her hands fell to his waist and began to unfasten his pants. Their lips locked, their tongues sliding together in a long, moist kiss. Alex's strong hands moved up and down the voluptuous body, feeling the soft curves of her hips, the small of her back, her large breasts.

"Give it to me," she said, pulling her open mouth away from his. She pulled him toward the bed, pushing his pants down. Somehow her slinky dress opened at the side, revealing dark thighs.

Hopelessly entwined, they fell together onto the bed with Nanos on top. The flowers perched on the side of her head fell askew, and her long black hair flowed across the sheets like dark glistening water. The former Miss Uruguay shivered with desire and breathed in short, quick gasps. Nanos broke from her lips and moved down her body, burying his face in the warm flesh of her breasts.

He felt her stiffen slightly as she drew her breath.

"Aleek," she whispered hotly into his ear. She moved her legs under the weight of his body and suddenly jerked her knee up, ramming him in the crotch.

The Greek gasped as the excruciating pain ripped violently through his body. Weak and openmouthed in shock, he looked up just as she drew a five-inch hatpin from the orchids tangled in her hair. With a vicious smile, she thrust it straight toward his right eyeball.

4

Barrabas lifted the Browning to the level of the open car window.

"Slow right down, Hermann! Let them think we're going to stop. And get down!" he instructed the Swiss. Both men slouched low in the seats until they could barely peer over the dashboard. Hermann braked the Spider.

"Listen carefully and do exactly what I say," Barrabas said urgently. "Put it in low gear."

The attorney tugged the gearshift and slipped it into second. Barrabas kept one eye on the Renault as they approached. With his other eye, he watched the needle on the speedometer sink. The occupants of the black car opened the doors on the side facing away from them. Hermann's sports car slowed to less than twenty-five kilometers an hour. Two men wearing green windbreakers jumped into position behind the Renault. Small black objects in their hands indicated they were well armed.

"Okay, Hermann. Turn a little to the left and floor it. Hit the fuckers just above the rear wheel and don't stop."

Hermann gasped, momentarily uncertain.

"Hermann!" Barrabas shouted again.

The Swiss attorney stiffened, depressed the accelerator all the way and geared up. The Spider zipped forward, its velocity rapidly increasing.

The attackers behind the Renault froze momentarily, questioning their own perceptions. Then they ran for it. Too late.

The front right fender of the Spider curled like an accordion, shattering the headlight. The impact threw Barrabas and Heinzmuller toward the dash. The rear end of the Renault slid across the road, pushing the car into the building on the corner.

Heinzmuller wound the steering wheel to the left, pulling the Spider onto the esplanade and accelerating on the road along the bank of the Rhône River.

Barrabas looked back. One of their attackers was definitely down—pinned under the wheels of the Renault and thrashing like an overturned beetle. The other had fallen into a crouch, his right arm stretching forward into a firing position.

"Down, Hermann." Barrabas quickly turned, slouching into his seat. The back window splintered, and two bullets pounded into the aluminum plates behind the seats like whacks from a crowbar.

Hermann kept his foot on the gas pedal, not turning or speaking until the roadblock was almost a kilometer behind them. A high-pitched chuckle escaped his throat.

"This is incredible," he muttered, shaking his head.

"What I'd like to know is whether they're your friends or mine," Barrabas mused, twisting in the seat as he looked around for more pursuers. Someone was engaging in some fairly sophisticated parallel surveillance of Hermann Heinzmuller's Spider. And they weren't finished yet. A lime-green Citroën turned onto the esplanade. It was coming up behind them too fast to be part of the normal traffic.

"It's not over," Barrabas told his attorney.

The Citroën pulled into the left lane in an effort to pass. "What should I do, Nile?" Hermann asked, glancing in the rearview mirror. He was beginning to take it all in stride.

"Roll down your window, and when they pass our taillights, brake right to the floor."

Hermann quickly opened the window as Barrabas watched the oncoming car. There were two people in the front seat. The small metallic barrel of a gun suddenly protruded from the passenger's side just as the Citroën reached the Spider.

"Now!" Barrabas shouted.

Hermann changed pedals and slammed his foot to the floor. The brakes squealed, and the Citroën suddenly shot up parallel to the driver's seat of the Fiat. Barrabas reached past Heinzmuller's face with the Browning gripped firmly in his hand and fired.

The 9 mm parabellum knocked into the gunman, opening a big red smile where his nose had been.

Blood and brains sprayed over the driver. The car passed them, swerving wildly. The gunman's weapon dropped onto the road as the man's body slumped over the window, shaking like a rag doll and dripping gore.

The roadway along the Rhône had left the central area of Geneva and had entered parkland. On one side there was a two-meter stone embankment. On the other an iron fence ran along the edge of the river. The swiftly moving waters were dangerously high from heavy winter rains. There were no exits from the esplanade for at least a kilometer.

"Pull over, Hermann! Fast! I'm driving."

"We got those bastards!" Hermann shouted defiantly, taking one hand off the wheel to shake his fist.

The Swiss attorney brought the Spider to a screeching halt in the middle of the road. Barrabas jumped out before it stopped moving, ran around the car and flung open the door.

"Forgive me, old friend." He grabbed Heinzmuller by the lapels of his coat and yanked him from the driver's seat. "I'll be back for you."

He jumped into the car and floored the accelerator, leaving his lawyer gasping and speechless at the side of the road.

The driver of the Citroën regained control and a half-kilometer lead. But the tables were turned. The hunter was now pursued by his quarry.

The souped-up carburetor on the little sports car performed well, giving Barrabas a speed of more than ninety kilometers an hour in less than fifteen seconds. The speedometer kept climbing, and the gap between the Spider and the Citroën quickly narrowed. The rear end of the lime-green car came up fast.

Barrabas aimed straight for it, swerving slightly to the left at the last minute. He slammed the Citroën to the right of the left taillight and braked slightly to draw back. The rear end of the Citroën fishtailed as the tires slid sideways from the impact. The car headed toward the river. Barrabas jammed on the brakes again as the escaping car turned almost ninety degrees, blocking the roadway.

At the last moment the driver regained control. The tires screeched as he leveled it and accelerated.

Barrabas wasn't finished. He veered into the left lane and pulled forward, edging past the Citroën's rear bumper. The driver of the French car zigzagged madly, forcing the American to slacken his speed.

The roadway curved. The headlights of an oncoming car appeared just as Barrabas pulled through an opening and paralleled the Citroën. He braked and swerved right as the approaching driver hit his horn. The car tore past. Barrabas pulled into the left lane again.

For the second time he edged ahead of the Citroën, and with a sharp right twist of the steering wheel bashed the front of the Spider into the escaping car. Once again the car's rear wheels slid sideways, and the Citroën headed toward the guardrail along the river.

Barrabas decelerated and countersteered to break contact.

Sparks flew along the guardrail as the Citroën's front fender scraped it. The car fishtailed, bashing the right side into the hard wall. Still the driver maintained control, pulling the car back into the center of the roadway.

"Sheeit," Barrabas cursed. He had no alternative. He pressed the accelerator. The Spider's engine roared as the little sports car overtook the damaged Citroën. As Barrabas passed the driver, he saw the man's face, white and scared.

"You ain't seen nothing yet," he muttered. He waited until the center of the Spider was even with the front bumper of the Citroën. Then he gave a repeat performance, steering sharply to the right and hitting the front left corner of the lime-green car. From that angle the full weight of the little sports car was no match for the larger Citroën. The attacker had no way to go but right—into the Rhône.

The Citroën shattered the iron guardrail and tumbled through the air. It did a perfect nosedive and sank immediately beneath the cold, treacherous waters of the swollen river.

"WELL, WHADDYA KNOW," O'Toole said, staring across at the little dark eye that was the killing end of Ted Merkin's gun. "And I didn't bring mine."

"It won't be necessary," Merkin said, only slightly amused. "Now if you'll be good enough to stand up and accompany me to the washroom. It will be much easier for the cleaning staff to wash down the tile than if we make a mess on the carpet here. And inevitably it will be messy. You know how these things are, I'm sure."

O'Toole picked up a pencil from Merkin's desk and tapped it nervously against the palm of his other hand. "Do I get an explanation? I mean this is quite an elaborate setup you've got here. You must want me badly."

"An explanation would only be time-consuming, Mr. O'Toole. And my instructions were brief and to the point. In a few minutes you won't even care. Let me just say that Crow Books has never heard of you, your book, or me for that matter."

He stood up behind the desk, keeping his pistol leveled carefully at the Irishman. His voice turned cold.

"Now get up."

O'Toole sighed. He tucked the pencil behind his ear and stood.

"Put your hands over your head, turn around and walk straight ahead. You'll see the washroom door near where you came in. Proceed very slowly. I'm not averse to soiling the carpet if there's no other way."

O'Toole went across the open office space with Merkin right behind him, pressing the barrel of the handgun into the small of his back. The washroom door had been removed from its hinges. O'Toole walked inside.

There were three toilet stalls, the same number of urinals and a row of sinks in the narrow gray-tiled room.

"Inside," Merkin ordered, motioning with his gun toward the last stall. "Get down on your knees and put your head over the toilet."

"Sure we can't negotiate?" O'Toole ventured, pushing against the door to the stall. He scratched the side of his head, carefully slipping the pencil into his hand. He wedged the eraser into his palm and closed his fist around it. The sharpened end protruded between the base of his second and third fingers.

"Positive," Merkin said.

O'Toole turned like lightning, his left arm knocking Merkin's pistol away from the small of his back. With his right, he aimed the pencil for a small spot on the side of Merkin's neck, just below his chin.

O'Toole drove it hard. The sharpened point pierced the assassin's flesh like a push dirk, driving up into his mouth and through his soft palate. With his left hand, O'Toole grabbed Merkin's wrist, forcing him to hold the pistol to the side.

Merkin howled with sudden gruesome anguish, his face and eyes frozen in shock. He drew his head back, slamming it against the tile wall. The instinctive recoil gave O'Toole exactly the angle he needed and stabilized his target.

He plunged the pencil in until his fist slapped against Merkin's jawbone. The deeply embedded point pierced brain matter.

Merkin stiffened. His fingers curled, squeezing the trigger on the gun. It fired harmlessly, blowing a hole in the metal wall of the toilet stall and ricocheting off the tile floor. The assassin's eyes suddenly became very peaceful, almost happy, and the corners of his lips twitched into a smile. His body shuddered briefly and collapsed on top of O'Toole's spiked fist.

O'Toole extricated his hand from the pencil and pushed the corpse farther into the stall, letting it slump over the toilet. Quickly he checked the dead man's pockets. They were empty. He slipped the gun into his pocket, grabbed a handful of Merkin's hair and dropped his head into the toilet bowl.

"Drink up," O'Toole muttered. "No one calls my poetry crap and lives."

THE WAIL OF POLICE SIRENS grew louder in the distance as Barrabas watched the last few bubbles break the surface of the river. Headlights approached through the swiftly gathering dusk, and the cars of the Geneva police corps pulled up beside the parked Spider.

Hermann Heinzmuller was the first one out. He blanched at the sight of his little car. The front end was a write-off. Quickly he walked to the colonel and threw his arms around him.

"I forgive everything. You, my favorite client, are still alive. It was just like an American movie," he added incredulously.

In the questioning that followed, the Swiss police conveniently assumed that Hermann Heinzmuller was the principal target of an attempted kidnapping and ransom plot. It was a common method for European extremists to raise funds to finance their terrorist activities. Neither Barrabas nor the Swiss attorney said anything to dispel the official assumptions.

According to the police, the blue Peugeot and the black Renault had both disappeared. The terrorists had left nothing behind, except for some damaged cars at the first intersection and traces of blood on the pavement where the black Renault had tried to block them.

Night fell, broken by the flashing amber of the emergency barriers and the revolving cherries from the ambulance and police cars. The lights shone eerily across the wet pavement onto the cold gray waters of the Rhône.

Divers and a tow truck arrived. With a feverish efficiency typical of the Swiss, they quickly set about recovering corpses.

Barrabas and Heinzmuller stood to one side and watched silently as two divers emerged from the waves, gently floating the first of the bodies to shore.

It began to rain lightly. The colonel shivered against the fine cold drops and pulled his jacket tightly around him. Then he walked down the slippery riverbank to have a look. Hermann followed.

As the ambulance attendants unrolled the body bag and slipped it over the dead man's feet, Barrabas studied the face. The driver of the car had died with his eyes open. The dull brown irises looked resentful, as if the corpse remembered the awesome struggle against the cold asphyxiating waters of the Rhône. It was an Hispanic face. The skin had whitened in death, but the hair was black and the bone structure unmistakably Mediterranean. The man had been fairly young, perhaps in his late twenties.

"S'il vous plaît, monsieur," one of the ambulance attendants said softly, moving around Barrabas and Heinzmuller as he leaned to zip up the body bag. The dead man's arm suddenly flopped sideways, startling them.

Hermann gasped.

The marks on the underside of the dead man's arm were small but clearly visible—the twin lightning runes of the Nazi SS.

The ambulance attendant appeared not to notice. He thrust the arm back inside and zipped the bag up.

Barrabas and Hermann moved slowly away from the small crowd of police and medical personnel.

"I've seen this too often before," Hermann said. "Forty-five years ago in the camps. The SS didn't only tattoo numbers on the Jews. They also wore that sign on their own bodies to mark their brotherhood. But this man can't be true SS. He's too young. And he didn't appear German."

Barrabas watched silently as the body bag was lifted onto a stretcher and wheeled toward the waiting ambulance.

5

Geoff Bishop slid quickly to a halt beside Lee. He grabbed her jacket and pulled her up. Her skis swung by the safety straps from the ankles of her boots. Bishop squatted and unclipped them.

"Move into the woods on foot," he told her, "and climb uphill as fast as you can. I'll lead them off down the slopes."

"But—"

"Just do as I tell you. If one of them follows you, he'll have a helluva time climbing uphill unless he takes his skis off, too."

He handed her ski poles back to her. "Use these. They'll help you walk faster in the snow." Then he grabbed her skis and tucked them under his arm. "Go on!" he shouted.

Lee didn't want to, but she knew that she was a liability, slowing Geoff down. If the trick didn't work, maybe he at least would get away.

"I'll drop your skis near the woods farther down the hill. If they don't see your tracks, that'll give you extra time."

"Last one down," she said, smiling bravely.

"Last one down."

She kicked high to get her feet out of the snow-drifts as she ran, using the poles to push her forward. It made it easier, but by the time she reached the forest she was breathing hard. She kept running, putting another twenty meters between her and the ski run. There was a sudden drop-off where a frozen streambed had eroded the hillside. She jumped over the edge and looked back.

The men with the submachine guns appeared at the top of the ski hill. They stopped and surveyed the slopes. Lee held her breath.

One of the men said something. The other one nodded. They pushed off again, skiing down the slope. Hatton sank back with relief, giving herself a moment to catch her breath.

Then she froze. The attackers had stopped again. One of them skied close to the edge of the forest to look at the snow. He waved to the other one, who nodded again before continuing downhill.

The man by the forest quickly shucked off his skis and reached behind him to pull something off his back. A feeling of dread encompassed Lee when she saw what it was.

"Snowshoes," she murmured with horror. The man stooped down and quickly began to tie his boots into them.

She had to think of something fast.

Staying in the streambed, she wove as quickly as she could between the tangled branches of leafless willows. Wind had blown up snowdrifts almost waist high. She gasped painfully at the raw cold air, leaning for support against the trunk of a great white pine. Ten meters ahead, a huge old tree had fallen years earlier along the edge of the stream. She made her way to the dense thicket of bushes that had grown up around it. Carefully lifting her poles, she retraced her steps back to the pine.

She took one of her ski poles, straining to bend the aluminum alloy ninety degrees. She pushed it into the snow several feet from the pine beside her trail. Quickly she stripped off her jacket and stepped back to the pine tree, using the jacket to brush the snow over her tracks. Then she turned and threw the jacket so that it landed over the upright pointed tip of the ski pole.

With the other pole gripped firmly in one hand, she started climbing up the pine tree.

GEOFF BISHOP GRIPPED Lee's skis tightly under his arm, propelling himself with one pole down the slope. He made a fast curve onto a slight plateau, dropped the skis and kept going.

Twenty-five meters farther he stopped by the edge of the woods to wait.

A few moments later one of the attackers swooped onto the plateau. He saw the abandoned skis and came up quickly beside them.

Bishop cursed bitterly. There was only one. The diversion hadn't worked. He had no choice but to take care of this one as quickly as possible before going back to help Lee. He skied out of the forest onto the slope, long enough for his pursuer to see him. He dug a pole into the snow and spun around, skiing back into the woods and zigzagging through the trees. His attacker sent a hail of autofire after him, and bullets pounded into tree trunks, showering the white snow with bark and splinters.

Ahead of him, Bishop saw a hollow where a sheer granite rock face rose out of the snowdrifts like the back of a whale. Groundwater seeping down its sides had frozen into a wall of ice three meters high.

Bishop raced down the steep hill into the hollow, using his momentum to go up the far side. Halfway up, he spread his skis sideways, digging the edges into the side of the hill. Using the herringbone walk he climbed to the top and skied a short distance on the other side. Then he circled around to the top of the rock face. Silently he slipped his skis off. He dropped to his stomach and flattened himself on the ice, drawing close to the edge.

Soon Bishop saw his attacker enter the forest. The man proceeded warily, holding his small 9 mm submachine gun in ready position. Obviously a seasoned skier, the man used his legs and feet to control his skis and dragged his poles. For the first time, Bishop noticed the snowshoes strapped to the man's back.

Briefly his stalker stood at the edge of the hollow, surveying the woods and Bishop's tracks down the shallow hill and up the other side. He let go of the submachine gun, letting it swing from the strap around his shoulder, and grasped the handles of his poles. He dug them into the snow and pushed off.

Bishop leaped into a crouching position. His timing had to be fast and perfect.

The skier slid quickly into the hollow, gaining speed, and began the uphill slide, his momentum slowing.

Bishop pounced as swift and silent as a wendigo.

He landed hard on the man's back, throwing him facedown into the snow. The attacker's arms, trapped in the loops of the ski poles, were pinned underneath him. His legs twisted and caught in the long skis. He cried out. Something broke. Fiberglass or bone.

Applying total force, Bishop wrapped his left forearm around the man's neck, tightening it against his larynx and strangling the scream short. At the same time he drove his right forearm just under the crown of the man's head, instantly locking his left hand into the crook of his right elbow.

Snarling and clenching his teeth with savage determination, Bishop pulled his left arm toward him and jerked the man's head down. He jerked twice more.

In three seconds the unknown attacker's neck was broken. His last breath hissed from his limp body like air from an inflated doll.

Bishop recovered quickly.

Lee. He had to find her. He leaned over and tore the submachine gun and the snowshoes off the body. Quickly he flipped through the pockets in the ski suit, extracting a spare magazine and a hunting knife. As he expected, there was no wallet, no identification.

Feverishly he fastened his boots into the gut-and-leather snowshoes.

The blue sky and the beautiful winter day were gone. It had clouded over, and a few plump flakes of snow floated down.

Bishop checked the mag in the SMG. It was almost empty. He replaced it with one of the spares before working his way up the hill toward the ski run.

LEE HATTON DIDN'T HAVE to wait long. She stood on a thick limb of the pine tree four meters above the ground. Suddenly she heard the soft thumps of someone walking across the snow.

The killer appeared over the edge of the streambed, his SMG cocked and ready. The wide snowshoes floated almost on the surface of the powder, giving him the advantage of speed. He moved furtively, following her trail, but glancing around warily as if he expected a trick.

Hatton stopped breathing. Small piles of snow lay along the needled branches of the pine, and her slightest movement sifted it down. She watched as the killer approached. She had only one chance and she had to make it good. The killer saw her dark blue jacket and the trail leading to the fallen tree as soon as he climbed out of the streambed. He paused momentarily again before making his way to it, scanning the vicinity.

Hatton sucked in her bottom lip and bit down hard, silently begging the killer to take the bait.

He leaned over to pick up the jacket.

Lee dropped from the tree, holding her ski pole in front of her like a javelin. As the killer heard the noise, he dropped the jacket and looked up. He grunted as the sharp aluminum point of the ski pole drove through his body, piercing it on an angle from back to front. Lee swung sideways. She kept her grip on the makeshift spear, flipping the killer onto his back as she fell into the soft mattress of snow. The bent pole hidden in the snow protruded from his gut. She let go and rolled, grabbing her assailant's gun on the way by.

Now she was back in business.

The man screamed and thrashed his legs in desperate pain. His hands slipped along the bloody pole projecting from his chest as he attempted to pull it out. Suddenly he spewed blood from his ruptured lungs. He brought himself to his knees but faltered. More blood poured from his mouth, steaming onto the white snow.

Lee stood and ran back, training the gun on him. He looked at her with surprise in his eyes. It wasn't what he had expected from his day's work. His body went into a final death spasm and fell forward into the snow.

The ski pole stood at attention. Its rubber handle quivered for a moment. Then it stopped.

Winter silence returned to the Laurentian forest.

Lee shivered. Her coat, trapped under the body, was covered with blood, and she wore only a flannel shirt. It was snowing, starting to come down fast.

Behind her, from the direction of the ski run, she heard the soft thumps of snowshoes. She swung around, raising the SMG and tightening on the trigger.

Then she saw the familiar red-and-black ski suit. Geoff Bishop ran through the trees toward her, relief visible in his face. He glanced at the body. The crimson slush around it was freezing quickly.

"I impaled him," Lee said, her voice dull. She fell into Geoff's embrace, burying her face against his chest.

He felt her trembling from fear and the cold.

"It's okay. I took care of the other one." He pushed her away to unzip his suit. Underneath he wore a quilted jacket. He stripped it off and gave it to her.

"What happens now?" Lee asked, pulling it on, her teeth chattering.

"We talk to Barrabas. Something's going on."
He shrugged. "Or maybe I missed an alimony payment," he joked halfheartedly, then said, "Not funny."

Lee motioned toward the body. Already a fine layer of snow covered it. "What about him?"

"In another hour he'll be frozen and buried in the snow. In the spring someone might find some bones or whatever's left that the animals haven't eaten or dragged away."

Lee shivered again. "First one down, okay?"

"First one down what?"

"First one down gets into a real hot bath."

"Why don't we both get in together?"

Lee's eyes brightened. This time she laughed a little, her spirits starting to return. "We deserve it, if you ask me."

As they left the forest, Geoff Bishop looked back once. A shiver climbed his spine from the terror that had struck them on a beautiful day in the placid Canadian woods.

IN ONE BRIEF MILLISECOND Alex Nanos realized he was going to die. The former Miss Uruguay's five-inch pin was about to pierce his eyeball and go straight through the center of his brain. He screamed.

"Billieeeeee!"

As if by magic, the former Miss Uruguay suddenly rose horizontally from the bed and floated in midair.

Billy Two towered over the bed, holding her aloft. His mighty hand clenched the wrist of the hand that held the deadly pin.

Another lucky day for the Greek. Then all hell broke loose.

The ex-Miss Uruguay screamed like a banshee.

Alex rolled off the bed and tried to grab her. She kicked at him, jabbing her stiletto heels into his face and kicking him in the jaw.

She swiped her free hand across Starfoot's face, slicing five livid red wounds down his cheek. He tried to grab the other arm, but she moved too fast, twisting, kicking, turning and screaming like a cat on fire. She twisted her hand and dug the pin into Billy Two's arm.

His eyes went white, and his teeth snapped together as the pain rippled up to his shoulder.

This was no lady.

He dug his hand into her silver lamé dress and grabbed the slithery material. Holding the struggling wild cat as far away from him as possible, he ran through the open door to the balcony and threw her over the edge.

She screamed all twenty-six stories on the way down.

The scream was punctuated by a sharp, slapping sound. Then there was silence.

Nanos and Starfoot looked at each other, then ran to the balcony and looked over the edge.

"That's one assassination attempt that fell flat on its face," Billy Two commented.

"Billy, that was the greatest defenestration I ever saw," Alex murmured in amazement. Starfoot looked incredulously at the Greek. "Defenestration? Alex, where did you learn a word like that?"

Nanos shrugged. "I dunno. It means getting thrown out a window. You think I'm stupid or something? I can't speak American?"

"Me think you're stupid? Not at all, Alex. I mean, you're the one who brought her up here, aren't you? Besides, I didn't throw her through a window. I threw her off the balcony."

"Same difference, Billy. What do we do now?"

"Check out."

Alex nodded. "Like fast."

"Like now."

6

The towers of Manhattan were wreathed in fog, and the city basked in a damp midwinter thaw that brought with it occasional patches of gray drizzle.

"Just watch, tonight the temperature will drop to below zero. The whole town will turn into a giant skating rink. I tell ya, whatta way ta make a livin'." The talkative taxi driver spoke over his shoulder, looking at Barrabas through the Plexiglas window separating the front seat from the back. He chattered most of the way from John F. Kennedy Airport into Manhattan, weaving in and out of the New York City traffic by instinct.

Barrabas reached into the front seat and pressed thirty bucks into the driver's hand as they slowed in front of a midtown skyscraper.

"Keep the change," he said. "And have a good one."

"Hey! Thanks, buddy. You, too."

Barrabas slammed the door and walked quickly across the wide granite plaza toward the glass doors that led to the lobby. Inside the stainless-steel elevator, he pressed sixty-four and inserted a small plastic card with a magnetic strip into a slot below the buttons. A bell rang softly. The doors closed, and the elevator effortlessly ascended.

The sign reading Walker Jessup Agency, International Consultants was at the end of the corridor. Once again he inserted his card into the slot beside the door. The lock buzzed, and he pushed through into a sterile corridor lit by a long fluorescent light. At the end double steel doors were tightly closed. Above them a video camera whirred as it rotated in his direction. A disembodied computer voice—female, and almost seductive—instructed him from a nearby intercom, "Please proceed to the next door and insert your security card."

It was a routine he had followed dozens of times, and he barely listened. The only difference was the low, even vibrations that seemed to come from the other side. After inserting his card, a red light above the metal slot lit up while the computer read the magnetic tape.

"Thank you, Mr. Barrabas. You may proceed."

The double doors slid back with a whisper.

The assault of full-volume disco music was something he was utterly unprepared for. A young man sat behind a semicircular console, feet up, reading a newspaper with a splashy pink-and-yellow cover.

He had short dark hair, cut to military length. But the resemblance to the armed forces ended there. He wore a crumpled shirt that looked like a pajama top and had a crucifix dangling from his ear. The dark horn-rimmed glasses perched on the edge of his nose were obviously for decoration only, since there was no distortion of his face behind them. A black cord, the kind matronly shopwomen wore, hung from each arm of the spectacles and draped around the back of his neck. A ghetto blaster sat beside the console of video monitors along the desk.

Barrabas flicked the music off.

The young man jumped forward in surprise, suddenly noticing the tall man standing over him. He dropped the newspaper and swung his legs off the desk.

"Er, sorry, sir. What can I—"

"Nile Barrabas to see Walker Jessup. He's not in, is he?" Aside from the relaxed state of Jessup's current secretary, the door to the Fixer's office stood ajar, and his long desk of polished granite was empty.

"No, sir. Left the country three days ago, sir."

Despite his appearance, the young man answered with the crisp ring of military experience.

"Where is he?"

The secretary shook his head. "He didn't say, sir. All he said was to hold the fort until he got back."

"Did he give you instructions on what to do if he didn't return?"

The young man shook his head. "No, sir. He was in a very good mood when he left. He said...well..."

"What?"

"He said it was the easiest one point six million dollars he ever made. Then—" the secretary seemed almost embarrassed, and Barrabas waited "—he was sort of singing as he went out the door. 'Wine, women, song, food, especially food.' It sounded to me like he was taking a vacation. But there was a message for you that someone left yesterday."

"For me?" Barrabas was surprised.

"Yes, sir. It was left with the message service when the office was closed for lunch. Whoever it was didn't say who called. Just that they were looking for Nile Barrabas. You know phone services, sir. They're not very reliable."

The colonel thought a moment. There were very few people who knew of the connection between him and the Fixer, and those that did would have asked for Jessup, not him.

"Uh, sir?" the young man asked cautiously. "Are you the Colonel Nile Barrabas, formerly of the Fifth Special Forces Group Airborne, First Cavalry Division?"

Barrabas nodded. "That's me. How'd you know?"

A smile broke across the young man's face. "That's my old company, sir. Four years. You're still a legend around there. The last American soldier out of Vietnam, and you didn't even show up to collect the Medal of Honor from the president himself! Former Corporal Jimmy Ducett. It's an honor to meet you, sir!"

Barrabas smiled in spite of himself, gave a casual salute and turned toward the door.

"If Walker returns, should I tell him you were looking for him?" the young man asked. He pushed a button on the console, and the double doors parted smoothly.

"It won't be necessary. I'll find him first." Barrabas headed through the doors into the long sterile corridor again. Abruptly he stopped and looked back at Jessup's secretary. "Corporal Ducett, what's with all the..."

The former grunt looked puzzled.

The colonel motioned to his hair and clothing.

"Oh, that!" the young man said, smiling in comprehension. He shrugged as if nothing was out of the ordinary. "New York."

By THE TIME BARRABAS HAD rented a car and driven to the freeway leading north out of the city, the fine drizzle had turned into a determined cold winter rain. Visibility was down to almost nil, and traffic to Connecticut soon lined up bumper to bumper.

There were two things that Jessup's assistant had told him that didn't make sense. First, the Fixer didn't take vacations. At least he never had in all the time that Barrabas had known him. And second, no matter what mood Jessup was reportedly in when he left his office, no one earned one million six hundred thousand bucks easily.

Adding the two things together, it was clear the big Texan had gone off on an assignment somewhere. Since Jessup had left the CIA, he never did anything personally dangerous. For those kinds of missions he hired Barrabas. Eventually, in a few days or a few weeks, the Fixer would show up. But Barrabas wanted him now.

Barrabas had no doubts that the attack in Geneva was aimed at him. Hermann Heinzmuller was too unimportant and too easy a target for the kind of parallel surveillance that had been mounted against them. Now he wanted to know who was after him, and why.

Walker Jessup had the international resources to find out. And the only possibility Barrabas had of finding him was through Nate Beck, the SOBs' computer genius.

The traffic didn't begin to clear until after New Haven, and by that time the dark rainy day had turned into just plain darkness. The red taillights of the cars ahead of him gleamed like neon strips on the rain-slicked asphalt. Heavy drops exploded into shards of light on the windshield. The defroster on the rental car was almost completely inadequate to the task, and Barrabas had to keep wiping the windshield with his hand to maintain visibility.

Fifty miles later, near the old whaling port of Mystic, he turned off I-95 onto a secondary road that led east toward the state line with Rhode Island. It took him almost another hour of slow driving before he found the country road leading through the forest to the coast. Several miles farther on, the old beach house came into view, the windows blazing with light through the pouring rain. He stopped the car by the steps leading up to the front porch and pulled his collar up to make the three-meter dash to the veranda. The howling wind and the crashing of the North Atlantic waves on the nearby beach seemed to heighten the fury of the storm.

He pressed the doorbell.

Although the curtains were drawn across the wide bay windows on either side of the front door, Barrabas could see inside through small diamond panes in the door itself.

Nate was obviously home. There was a bank of computer screens lined up in front of consoles on a long table in the living room, and a freshly stoked fire burned invitingly in the fireplace.

After waiting several minutes, he pressed the bell again. No answer. He walked down the length of the veranda, peering around the sides of the house. There was a new Buick parked near the garage, and down by the beach there was a dune buggy. He went back to the front door and pressed the bell again. Then, for the second time in as many days, he reached inside his jacket and slipped the Browning from its holster.

The handle turned easily. The wind caught the door, throwing it open and ripping through the room, scattering papers in the living room and blowing a hall lamp over. Barrabas caught it before it fell, grabbed the door and pushed it closed against the force of the winter squall. He moved slowly into the front hall, stepping softly and listening carefully. The dining room on his right was dark and empty. He turned left into the living room that ran the length of the house. He could hear a low hum from the computers and the crackling of wood burning in the fireplace. Several of the computer screens displayed data, and half a glass of beer sat by one of the consoles. He followed the wires leading from the side port to a modem and the telephone. He looked at the screen.

The data was scrolling upward as lines appeared rapidly at the bottom. What he read at first struck him as a little odd.

Sexy girl, all alone in cold Wisconsin winter. Twenty-three and primed for warming up.

Hi, sexy girl. I love Wisconsin. Want to talk?

The data on the rest of the screen was in the same vein. It looked like some kind of computer dating service.

A doorway at the end of the room led to the back of the house, and Barrabas edged toward it, keeping his back to the wall. There was another dark hallway, and beyond he could see the light on in the kitchen.

Still there was no sight or sound of Nate Beck.

He slipped into the hallway, turning his gun around to hold it as a club. He heard a slight rustling and sensed someone invisible in the darkness. Something jumped from the shadows. Barrabas lashed out, smashing the butt of the pistol into the head of the silent attacker.

NOT FAR FROM WASHINGTON, D.C., in the wood-paneled study of a Georgetown mansion, the senator pored over briefing papers at his desk. The elderly invalid clutched the arm of his wheelchair and felt for the controls. The electric motor whirred, and he glided across the floor to the fireplace and hurled a handful of papers into the flames.

"Better no one sees these," he muttered, brushing long, thin strands of his white hair away from his eyes. He clasped his gnarled hands together and watched the documents burn.

The senior senator was the head of the secret House Committee that oversaw highly sensitive covert action—an unpleasant but necessary part of American foreign policy. The committee thought up the assignments. Barrabas did the dirty work. The only links between the politicians and the mercenary were the senator on one side and Walker Jessup on the other.

Despite the valuable unrecognized work accomplished by Barrabas and his commandos, who were felt to be indispensable to the U.S. government, the senator was Barrabas's sworn enemy.

An antique clock over the fireplace chimed five times. Precisely as the last chime ended, the door at the far end of the room opened. A young heavily made-up brunette entered. Her thin wool dress hugged the curves of her body.

"Time for your medicine now, Senator," Miss Roseline said demurely, like a governess talking to a little child. "And then your five-fifteen appointment will be here." A paneled door behind the desk led to a kitchenette. She stooped to take several small bottles of medicine from the tiny refrigerator.

The whirring electric motor of the wheelchair was her only warning. She dodged just as the senator glided behind her with the sole aim of putting his hand up her dress. Clutching the medicines in one hand, she slapped the ancient claw away.

"Now, now, Senator. We know that we're not supposed to do that. We already decided that when you're in the mood for that, we call one of those nice girls from the agency, since that's their job. My job is to take care of you and give you your medicine."

"Baah!" the senator snarled grumpily. "It wasn't intended that way when I hired you, Miss Roseline."

"Perhaps not, Senator. But that's the way it is now."

The young brunette busied herself mixing the medicines in a glass. The senator watched, his resentment and frustration building.

Miss Roseline was the last in a long line of curvaceous secretaries who had withstood the test of his pawing hands and searching lips. They hadn't been hired for their typing skills. Since his unfortunate accident, however, the senator required more extensive services.

He'd tried almost a dozen women, but sadly Miss Roseline was the only one who was competent enough to ensure that his strict medical regimen was followed. It was sad because she also refused to provide him with the sexual favors his previous secretaries had accustomed him to. The senator hated her for it. But no longer could he live without her. Unlike the others, she hadn't tried to murder him with overdoses of his own medicine. At least not so far.

Miss Roseline handed him a glass of foaming green liquid. "Now drink up," she said with sugary sweetness and a condescending smile.

The senator curled his lip in distaste and took the glass. It tasted awful.

"I'll kill him," he muttered, forcing down mouthfuls of the noxious liquid. "I'll see him dead in hell."

"What was that?" The secretary gripped the handles of the wheelchair and pushed the senator to the warmth of the fireplace.

"Barrabas. Nile Barrabas! You don't know who I mean, anyway. He's the one who's responsible for putting me in this wheelchair. I'll have his balls for it. Mark my words."

"Mmmm. I thought Jeremiah, that mad cult leader, was the one who broke your back when he attacked you." The young woman moved to the window and pushed the white curtains together, closing out the fast-growing winter dusk.

The senator clammed up and muttered inarticulately, torn between the temptations of letting loose his rancor and giving away state secrets. Or his own secrets. It was true that Jeremiah, a giant with Rasputin-like powers over his followers, had been directly responsible for paralyzing him from the waist down. But he had also been an important financial contributor to the senator's reelection.

If Barrabas hadn't set out, against orders, to destroy Jeremiah, the senator wouldn't have had to go to the cult leader's jungle camp to warn him. He would never forget that terrible day. When Jeremiah found out that his plan to take over Central America was imperiled by a small team of mercenaries, he picked the senator up and broke him over his knee like a twig for a bonfire.

"I hate him," the senator uttered coldly. He gulped back the last of his medicine.

"Now, now," Miss Roseline murmured, patting his shoulder. "The medicine will calm you." She soothed him by kneading his shoulders, knowing full well that the side effects of the concoction transformed him from a cynical egomaniac to a maudlin fool. In half an hour the senator, weeping and mourning over life's miseries, would be a pathetic sight to behold. She checked her watch. Time for the five-fifteen.

She left the senator to mutter at the burning logs in the marble fireplace and crossed the room toward the door. It opened before she got there. In the entrance stood a thin man with a tiny bemused smile playing across his pallid face. He wore an expensive suit, and his winter coat was draped across his arm. His hair was short on the sides but long on top and carefully slicked back. Miss Roseline stopped. She felt his dark eyes flicking up and down her body in a careful appraisal.

"Mr.—"

"Never mind," he interrupted. "I'm here to see the senator." His face darkened. "We have some business to discuss."

The old man in the wheelchair twisted around to see his visitor.

"Come in, David," he said loudly. "Pull up a chair."

As the visitor crossed the room to the senator, Miss Roseline turned back to the kitchenette and began to put away the bottles of medicine.

"Leave those for now, Miss Roseline," the senator called to her from the study. "And leave us in private."

The secretary paused, carefully setting the bottles on the counter. Another door led from the kitchenette to a storage room, which in turn gave access to another room in the mansion. Quickly she slipped the bolt open. Then she returned to the study, closing the door to the kitchenette behind her.

"Is that all for the day?"

"Yes, that's fine, Miss Roseline," the senator dismissed her.

The two men watched silently as she left the study and closed the door tightly behind her.

The younger man threw his coat over a chair and reached inside his suit jacket for a sheaf of telexes in the inner breast pocket. He summarized the contents of each as he tossed them one by one into the fire. His lips were tight with anger that he did little to conceal.

"From Interpol. Terrorists attack a wealthy attorney in Geneva. Both the attorney and the client who was with him escape. Three of the attackers are dead. The former Miss Uruguay plunges to her death from a hotel in Acapulco this morning. This afternoon the Quebec Provincial Police are asked to investigate a leased car abandoned at a ski resort in the Laurentians. The car is full of weapons and ammunition. The lessees—who happened to be agents of the Black International—don't show up. Let's put two and two together, Senator. This Nile Barrabas and his team of mercenaries—all of them—have slipped through our grasp again!"

The senator tightened his fist and bashed it against the arm of his wheelchair, accidentally sideswiping the controls. The chair jerked forward into the fireplace, throwing a shower of sparks over the carpet and into his lap. The senator yelped and hit the reverse button. He slapped at the sparks smoldering on his blanket as he backed up.

The young man watched, slightly contemptuous. He didn't lift a finger to help.

"Damn him! Damn him to hell!" the old politician roared, clutching his temples. His face was crimson with anger, and the veins on his forehead threatened to pop. "We'll never get him! Never! I already told you that!"

The senator's mysterious visitor paced. "We failed once already, with X Command. But those Florida fools weren't professionals. The network of the Black International includes the finest assassins in the world. They owe us for favors in connection with the upcoming Bolivian matter. They can bloody well try again."

"How?" the Senator demanded disparagingly. "Especially now that Barrabas and his people have been alerted by the failure of these so-called invincible agents." Suddenly the invalid's mood changed. "It's hopeless," he said, wiping a tear away from the corner of one eye.

The visitor seemed not to notice.

"Not yet. I know exactly what his next step will be. He'll go running for Walker Jessup in New York City. Fortunately my agents have already removed the Bolivia file."

"But you told me part of it was missing. The list of contacts, the plans for the takeover—"

"As long as Barrabas doesn't get hold of it, he won't interfere with our South American friends and their plans. That fat slob Jessup probably took it with him to La Paz."

The senator's eyes clouded with tears, and the corners of his mouth sank like a ship kissed by an iceberg.

"Poor old Jessup," he wept. "I didn't want him to die.

"Don't be an old woman about it," the senator's guest said sharply. "Jessup was a slob and a fool and in the way. It's a bit too late now for regrets, isn't it, Senator?"

The old politician sniffled. "But you didn't know him. I did. He used to come into this office and sit in that chair. Right in front of me. Even if I didn't like him, I knew him. It's different if death is just a statistic, a button or a vote in Congress, or some troublemaker with no real face. But when you know the target, it's so . . . sordid."

The invalid shuddered.

The flustered visitor looked at the suddenly soft-hearted senator in stupefied amazement.

"I can't believe you. I . . . I think you need your medicine, Senator." He cleared his throat and picked his coat up from the chair where he had thrown it. "In any event, we haven't given up yet. I'll let you know what happens. Good evening, Senator. I'll find my own way out."

Behind the paneled door to the kitchenette, Miss Roseline quickly stood and retreated through the other door into the storage room. She stepped carefully over boxes and mops and exited from the closet into the front hall barely before the senator's visitor left the study.

"You'd better do something for him," the young man said smoothly as his eyes made a return voyage across the woman's curves. "He's not quite right."

"I'll check on him right away."

She showed the visitor to the door. A long black limousine waited for him in the front drive. When he was gone, she went quickly to her own office, a small room just off the foyer of the old Georgetown mansion. She spun the Rolodex around to the *J* and flipped efficiently through the address cards until she came to the one she was looking for.

Jessup. Walker Jessup.

She picked up the phone and dialed.

7

The attacker yelped with pain and stumbled past Barrabas headlong through the doorway into the living room. He grabbed for the long drapes by the window and fell, dragging the curtains with him to the floor.

It was Beck.

"Shit!" the merc cursed, rolling in a tangle of cloth, pulleys and curtain rods and holding his head with his other hand. "Jeez!"

"What in hell were you doing, Nate?" Barrabas demanded as he extended an arm and helped Nate to his feet. Beck pulled rolls of curtain material away from his legs and arms.

"Colonel, you're the last person I expected out here," the short dark-haired man said, still wincing from the pain. He pulled his hand away from his forehead. There was a distinct two-inch-long purple bruise growing more livid by the moment. "Is there blood?"

Barrabas shook his head. "Do you always hide in there when people come to the door?"

"It's Beverley, Colonel. My ex-wife has tried turning me in twice so far. And I know the way she thinks. Three times lucky. I live in terror. You don't know what it's like."

Barrabas had recruited Nate Beck after a scam in which he'd used his computer genius to steal a million dollars by skimming the nickels and dimes from millions of bank accounts. His vindictive wife, Beverley, had used the scam as an excuse to turn him over to the police. Barrabas had arrived at Beck's European hideout barely minutes ahead of Interpol.

Of all the SOBs, Beck had had the least combat experience. His military career had been spent mainly in military research, designing electronic communications systems and eventually devising sophisticated codes for intelligence agencies. But what he lacked in experience, he made up for in enthusiasm.

The diminutive Jew from Queens, New York, was a genius with computers but lived in a swashbuckling Errol Flynn dreamworld. His recruitment to the SOBs had been an opportunity beyond his wildest imaginings. Occasionally the butt of good-natured jokes about his marksmanship and combat knowledge, he had worked hard at improving his abilities. Now he was considered an equal.

And his ability with computers went beyond genius. The guy was practically psychic with them.

"A terrible headache," Nate said, pointing to the bruise on his head. "You want coffee? I put some on just before I heard you drive up."

Barrabas nodded, and as Beck went into the kitchen, he sauntered back to the computer in the living room.

"What exactly are you working on, Nate?"

"Oh, that," Beck called from the kitchen. Thirty seconds later he appeared with two mugs of steaming coffee. He handed one to the colonel, and the two men sat in easy chairs. "It's a computer correspondence network. There are two channels, one's straight and one's for gays. You can communicate with chicks all over the country. If you see someone who looks interesting, you ask if they want to talk. Then you go into a private mode. At that point, the only limitation on what you do is the range of your fantasy."

"How do you know the woman you're talking to is what she says she is?"

"You don't. That's the beauty of it. Like I said, it's all fantasy stuff. I was just playing around. It gets a little lonely out here sometimes."

"You and Alex usually stick together when you're not on the job," Barrabas said. "Why isolate yourself out here?"

Beck laughed. "I love the Greek. He's a dynamo. He never stops. The women! The parties! Me? I need to stop sometimes. I wanted to spend some time hacking around with some of the new computer technologies they're coming out with. Besides, I hate Connecticut. It's the last place Beverley will think of looking for me. What brings you out here?"

Barrabas told him about the attack in Geneva and his urgent wish to track down Walker Jessup.

Beck sipped the hot coffee and appeared thoughtful as Barrabas spoke. "Sounds pretty straightforward to me. If he traveled by air, we check the passenger lists. If he used a credit card to pay for anything, we see what their computers can tell us. It'll take a few hours. I'll start now."

Barrabas looked at his watch. It was after nine. Three a.m. in Europe.

"I'm still suffering from jet lag a little. Mind if I get some shut-eye while you hack around?"

"No problem. You have your choice of four empty bedrooms upstairs. I'll call you when I come up with something."

Barrabas slept in the half-world between waking and unconsciousness, one eye peeled, one ear always listening. It was a soldier's instinct that made him sleep that way. He didn't know what time it was when Nate called some hours later. A quick glance at the luminous dial of his chronometer told him it was almost 4:00 a.m.

Nate stood at the door, his features in darkness, outlined by light from the hall.

"Colonel, it's not as easy as I thought. Can we talk?"

Barrabas rose quickly, instantly alert. He followed Beck downstairs.

"What is it?"

I've managed to access all the airlines, the major credit companies, Amtrak and the major car rentals. And so far I've come up with a big fat zilch.''

The three large computer screens in the living room were filled with masses of data—numbers and names from reservation lists.

"I thought maybe you'd know of an alias or something, or maybe have an idea of another tack to take."

Barrabas looked thoughtfully at the screens for a few moments.

"Yeah. Jessup always flies first-class. And he's too fat to fit into a single seat so he always books two. Does that give you something to go on?"

Nates face lit up. "Sure does!"

He sat at his chair, his hands suddenly flying over the keyboard. The data on the screens danced with names and numbers. Beck's face sank.

"Over a hundred airline seats were double-booked three days ago," he said. "And none of them Jessup."

"Who's this?" Barrabas pointed to one of the names on the screen. It was a famous cello player.

"The New York Philharmonic! Of course. Musicians with large instruments always take them on board with them. Those are economy seats, too. Let me get the first-class ones."

Once again the screen flickered. Now there were five names on it.

"That's a rock group called Dead Dictators," Beck said. "Four of them at least. That leaves one." He pointed at the screen. "D. Duck?"

Barrabas smiled. "That's it."

"As in Donald?"

"Porky Pig would have been more appropriate. Jessup has a weird sense of humor. I've seen him choose his aliases before."

"You sure?"

"No. Not totally. Let's see where Mr. Duck went." Beck typed in further instructions.

"Bolivia. Via Mexico City."

Barrabas slapped Beck on the back. "Congratulations!"

"You're positive?"

"Sure enough to wager a high roll."

BY MORNING THE RAIN AND DRIZZLE along the eastern seaboard had turned to wet snow. As usual there were no parking spaces to find in midtown Manhattan. Barrabas left Nate Beck to park his car and walked several blocks to the high white office tower that housed the Walker Jessup Agency, International Consultants, Inc. Fat wet snowflakes stuck to his sheepskin jacket and built into miniature little drifts, half melted on his shoulders and collar.

Liam O'Toole met him on the plaza in front of Jessup's building. The burly red-haired Irish-American brushed clumps of wet snow from his green duffel coat and stamped the gray slush off his big rubber galoshes. "Good to see you, Colonel," he said, extending his hand.

Barrabas had phoned Liam early that morning and had learned of the setup on him the day before.

"Have you talked to the others?" Barrabas asked.

O'Toole nodded. "Things got a little dicey when I talked to the desk of the hotel in Acapulco. It seems Alex and Billy checked out very quickly yesterday morning. But they wanted to know who I was, if I was a friend of theirs and especially if I knew where they could be reached. It seems the Mexican police want to talk to them about a beauty queen. The former Miss Uruguay apparently took a dive from their balcony twenty-six stories up. And she missed the swimming pool. I hung up."

"Sounds like a helluva party," Barrabas speculated.

"Yeah, well figure out for yourself what happened. Because I did get hold of Geoff Bishop and Lee Hatton in Montreal, and Canada's winter wonderland held some big surprises for them on the slopes yesterday. There were two of them, and both were eliminated. Geoff was very impressed with the submachine guns he's added to his collection. Very sophisticated 9 mm German-made Steyr Daimler Fuch. Someone had access to a good dealer."

"What about Claude Hayes?"

"He's been working on a project salvaging a seventeenth-century Spanish galleon that sank off the coast of Belize three hundred years ago. I caught him this morning. No problems. But he has his guard up now, and he's waiting to hear from us. What have you got so far, Colonel?''

"Bolivia."

"Bolivia? Someone in Bolivia's trying to get us all at once."

"No. Bolivia is probably where I'll find Walker Jessup. There are only a couple of possibilities for whoever's come after us."

"GRU?" O'Toole ventured. The Russian military secret police had a longstanding grudge against the team of American mercenaries.

"I don't think so. Remember I told you about the SS marks tattooed on one of the killers in Geneva. Nazis don't cavort with Communists. And vice versa. No, this goes back to Washington.

"We've known for a long time that someone on the House Committee is working against us. They've leaked information of our existence as a covert-action team before. But the only person who knew where we all were yesterday was the Fixer.

"I've known Jessup for years," Barrabas said. "He can spin webs around a tiger with his manipulations. But he wouldn't do this."

"Unless he was being forced to do it?" O'Toole suggested.

"That's a possibility. We won't know for sure until we talk to him. And so far, the trail leads to Bolivia. I'm hoping we'll find something more helpful in his files. Nate's parking the car. Can you wait for him before coming up? You know where it is?''

"Sixty-fourth floor," O'Toole answered as Barrabas disappeared through the revolving glass doors into the lobby of the skyscraper.

WHEN ALEX NANOS AWOKE, the hot tropical sun beat down on his face. A fly only slightly smaller than a B-52 was dive-bombing his nose, and he had a terrible ache at the base of his back from sitting up straight in the seat of the rattling old bus all night long.

He tried to open his eyes, but the lids were glued shut from the sleep and the heat. Just as well. The scenery would only be depressing. The fly droned persistently over his face and finally landed, its spiky little legs making his nose itch. He felt a sneeze building.

"Ah...ah...ah chooo!" His eyes popped open, and he flew forward in his seat.

Almost immediately a long, braying sound filled one ear, and he recoiled against the dank wet breath of a billy goat sitting in the aisle. The owner, a young Mexican boy, looked down at the Greek, his liquid brown eyes filled with a mixture of curiosity and amusement.

Nanos looked to his left. Billy Two was wide awake. He stared serenely out the window at the passing scenery—jungle that grew right to the edge of the road. Sometimes he hated the Osage. Times like now.

In the midst of total and utter misery, Billy Two managed to remain peaceful and relaxed. There was nothing Alex wanted more than to make the native American feel exactly the way he did —miserable.

"When do we get to the border?" he asked. His mouth felt like he had been chewing cotton balls all night long. Dirty cotton balls.

Billy Two flashed a smile.

"We passed an hour ago. We're in Belize."

"We're already in . . . How did that happen?"

"They weren't interested in our passports after I gave them fifty bucks."

"How much do we have left? Are we stopping for breakfast?"

"Alex, it was our last fifty bucks. We have nothing left."

Nanos groaned. Neither of them had eaten since their hasty exit from the hotel in Acapulco the previous morning, moments before the police and the hotel management had arrived at their door. It wasn't until they were on the street that they had realized that they had had less than a hundred bucks between the two of them. The American Express bureau was thick with policemen by the time they had gotten there, and the airport or train stations had been too risky to chance.

That had left them with one alternative. Their old buddy and fellow SOB Claude Hayes was in the neighboring country of Belize. They had had enough for the bus and some left over for bribes. Billy Two had commandeered their remaining money and had refused to spend a peso on food. Alex's stomach had shriveled to the size of a walnut and was beginning to collapse in on itself. And Billy Two seemed to enjoy it, almost thrive on it. Alex hated him. He vowed to make Starfoot miserable. One way or another.

The bus trip to Belize had been an unending dose of agony. Seven times they had changed buses as the ancient vehicles had rumbled from village to village. The roads were barely more than mud trails leading through the mountains of southern Mexico, down to the jungle of the Atlantic coast.

Their fellow passengers included an assortment of birds and animals normally found in barnyards. Half the time the two mercs had had to stand in the aisles, shoulders hunched and their heads pulled down to avoid hitting the ceiling. Billy Two had taken it all in stride, often smiling and chatting with the other passengers.

Toward midnight they had managed to commandeer two seats vacated by an old woman and the pig she was traveling with. Nanos had fallen quickly into a deep sleep, wondering what he'd done to deserve a lady with a five-inch hatpin.

"Look. See?" Billy Two said now, nudging him and pointing out the window. "We're almost there."

Through gaps in the jungle they could make out a forest of masts from the native fishing boats on a sandy beach. Beyond, the sapphire-blue water of the Caribbean sparkled invitingly.

Twenty minutes later the old bus pulled into the square of a small fishing village and stopped in front of a long wharf. A sixty-foot trawler was moored at the far end. Belize natives fished, and carried baskets of fruits and vegetables to the boats along the wharf.

"Where's Hayes?" Nanos moaned as he stepped out of the bus. He felt dizzy from not eating.

"Right there," Billy answered, pointing down the wharf.

"I don't believe it," Nanos muttered, squinting against the sun.

Claude Hayes was indeed on the wharf, talking to some people on the deck of the trawler. As if instructed by a sixth sense, the tall black American looked in their direction. He seemed momentarily puzzled, spoke quickly to someone on the trawler, then turned and began walking down the wharf.

He quickly recognized his buddies. With a broad smile and a wave, he broke into a run and joined them.

"What in hell brings you guys to this place? You want to join the salvage project?" he asked, after the men had greeted one another.

"We ran into a little problem in Acapulco," Starfoot began.

"And we were wondering if you could lend us a few bucks to buy breakfast," Nanos broke in. "Just until the local American Express office opens."

"You came all the way to Belize to borrow a few bucks," Hayes asked doubtfully, observing the pained expression in Alex's eyes. "What was this problem in Acapulco?"

Billy Two gave Hayes a quick rundown.

"How was I supposed to know she was kinky?" Nanos complained, looking around the square. "Is there a coffee shop? Breakfast specials? A few bucks just for a few hours, Claude, I swear."

"You two haven't been talking to the colonel?" Hayes asked slowly, searching their faces.

Both men shook their heads.

"Well, it seems there's been a little problem." Quickly he recounted his phone conversation with Liam O'Toole earlier that morning. "Nothing's happened around here," he concluded, "but I'm keeping my eyes open."

"We better report to New York," Starfoot suggested.

"After we eat," Nanos added. "Claude..." The Greek stuck his hand out, palm up. "Just a few bucks for breakfast?"

"Alex, the nearest American Express is two hundred kilometers away, and the only thing you'll find for breakfast down here is refried beans. And you wouldn't want to pay the price."

Nanos looked crestfallen. "What's that?"

"A week shitting your guts out in the latrine. My house is up there." Hayes pointed to a small bungalow nestled against the side of a low hill half a klick away. "How 'bout a good American breakfast of ham and eggs and some of my own special home fries?"

The Greek looked as if he'd pass out from delirium. "Lead on," he muttered.

Starfoot and Nanos followed the black man to an open Jeep near the wharf. As they drove through the dusty mud streets of the small village, Hayes explained the salvage operation.

"It's financed and run by a wealthy American guy. I used to take him on excursions when I ran that deep-sea fishing business in Nigeria. He claims we've found the wreck of the *Santa Rosa*, a Spanish galleon that sunk in a hurricane three hundred years ago. And if the historical records are right, there was about fifty million dollars' worth of gold and silver on board. So far we've found cannon, buttons, broken china and a few old doubloons. But no gold bars."

Just as Hayes pulled up in front of the little house, a tall thin man with East Indian features ran around the side of the house. He stopped abruptly, surprised to see the three men.

"Sabeel!" Hayes called, waving. "I have visitors. And they're hungry!" He turned to Starfoot and Nanos. "He's from the village—my chief cook and bottle washer."

Instead of greeting his employer, Sabeel looked frightened. He stepped back several feet, then suddenly broke into a run and fled on foot down the hill.

"That's strange. I wonder what got into him." Hayes watched him go with a puzzled expression. He looked at Billy Two.

Nanos stepped out of the Jeep and walked toward the house. "Is it locked?" he turned to ask Hayes, reaching out to twist the doorknob. It wasn't locked. The handle turned easily, and the door swung inward.

Billy Two and Claude Hayes looked at each other as the realization hit. The Osage turned and flung himself across the yard, tackling the Greek. The two men barreled sideways away from the house and rolled in the grass, propelled by the concussion waves of the enormous explosion.

The roof of the house lifted as the windows exploded into deadly shards. With a gushing roar, the entire frame building was consumed in flame.

O'TOOLE WAITED OUTSIDE the doors of the skyscraper, glancing around with occasional impatience and stamping the wet clinging snow from his feet and jacket. Words came into his head. He strung them along. They made a line. It was poetry. His muse was coming to him, as she always did, in times of *her* choosing, however inconvenient it might be for him.

Shoot while the ducks are flying, he told himself, reaching inside his jacket for a pen and something to write on. Quickly he scribbled down the words on the back of an automatic bank teller slip. He congratulated himself after he read it over:

A gambler says it's in the cards,
A woman says it's fate.
'Cause someday when you throw the dice
It's already far too late.
The salesman always gets his cut
Tho' your credit's good no more.
When the only deal in town is death
The dealer is a whore.

"I didn't know you wrote poetry." Nate Beck had approached unnoticed and was peering over O'Toole's shoulder.

O'Toole jumped. He quickly folded the paper and stuffed it into his pocket. His poetry was a very private affair.

"It was good," Nate said warmly.

"What's with you, you don't want to be recognized?" O'Toole demanded gruffly, anxious to change the subject.

Beck wore a dark trench coat, belted tightly at the waist. His face was almost obscured by the low brim of his hat and his dark sunglasses. His idea of incognito came from the TV late movies. One way or another, in New York, no one cared.

"Uh-uh. It's Beverley. My ex-wife. I know she's near here. I can feel her presence. Somewhere in a two-block radius. She's looking for me. And shopping."

"You're crazy, Nate."

"Never underestimate the psychic resources of a woman bent on vengeance." He shuddered. "And then there's Interpol. Where's the colonel?"

"Inside. Let's get out of this goddamn snowstorm before it becomes a blizzard.

"The two men walked across the wide granite plaza toward the front door. With the temperature dropping rapidly, the slush was turning to ice. The wind was picking up, driving snow crystals into their skin like little needles. A strong gust swept across the plaza just as they reached the doors, snatching Nate Beck's fedora and tossing it wildly away.

"Hey!" Nate shouted, grabbing for the hat and missing. "I'll meet you inside." He started running as the wind flipped his hat across the plaza.

Every time Nate reached his hat and bent down to pick it up, the wind teasingly snatched it away. Already the computer wizard was halfway across the wide expanse of granite.

Finally, for the third time, Nate caught up to it and plucked it from the wind's grasp just as it lifted off the ground again. He turned around and ran back toward the building. The slush had frozen into ruts and pools of ice. It made for slippery running, and more than once Beck's arms flew out for balance.

He didn't seem to notice the three men approaching him quickly from the side.

"Mr. Beck?" one of them called. The other two lurched forward just as Nate turned. His eyes widened, and he backed up. The man who had spoken whipped something from his pocket and flashed a badge. "Interpol."

Nate turned and made a beeline across the plaza. O'Toole watched the drama unfold from inside the lobby of the office building. It happened so fast that for a moment he couldn't believe his eyes. Nate was on the fly by the time O'Toole hit the revolving doors.

At the side of the building, the entrance to an underground parking garage cut into the plaza. Nate headed for it, scrambling over the metal railing. For a little guy who spent a lot of time working at a computer console he was surprisingly nimble.

A polished brown Jaguar emerged from the garage and drove up the incline toward the street. Nate jumped three meters to the ramp, landing in front of the driver's window. The owner of the Jaguar looked surprised and indignant.

Beck heard a whirring electronic noise. He looked up to see the metal door descending over the garage entrance. The perfect escape.

All he had to do was get there in time.

8

As Barrabas passed through the security to Jessup's inner office, he heard the heavy backbeat of a rap song blaring from within once again. When the door slid open, the young man at the desk quickly turned off the ghetto blaster. Today he wore a black studded leather vest and sported a blond zigzag through his hair.

He jumped to attention and saluted like a punk on parade.

"Colonel Barrabas! Is there anything I can do for you?"

"At ease, Ducett. We're not in the army now. You don't need to salute."

"Yes, sir." Ducett sat down slowly. "Still no word from Mr. Jessup, sir. But I have something that might interest you. I checked on that message that the phone service received. They keep the original notes that their operators scrawl down for thirty days, so I had them send over a photocopy." He opened a drawer in the desk and handed Barrabas a sheet of paper.

The operator had written "long distance," then "Mr. Jessup" in the "name of caller" space. "Jessup" had been scratched out and "Mr. Barrabas" written in.

"These phone services aren't very reliable," Ducett told him as he read it. "They get things scrambled up."

"What are you saying?"

"That maybe whoever called didn't ask for Mr. Jessup."

"Then maybe it *was* Jessup."

"Yeah. Asking for you."

Barrabas nodded thoughtfully. The kid was peculiar, but he had his head screwed on right.

"This came in for you, too." The young man handed Barrabas a telephone message slip. "She called last night just before I left. I don't know who she is, or how she knew you were coming here. But it sounded urgent."

Barrabas read it quickly. "Did it sound real?"

For a moment Jimmy Ducett didn't answer. Slowly he nodded. "Yeah, I'd say so, if I had to work on what my guts told me."

"What do you know about Bolivia?"

The Fixer's assistant looked sideways for a moment as he recalled by rote.

"One of two landlocked republics in South America, named for Simón Bolívar, the great military leader. Sandwiched by Peru, Chile, Argentina, Paraguay and Brazil, it has an area of 425,000 square miles, and a population of 5.2 million, most of whom live in the highlands and valleys of the Andes at an altitude—"

"Enough!" Barrabas put up his hands.

"I just researched it a few weeks ago for Mr. Jessup," the young man said proudly.

"I thought so. I want to see his file on Bolivia."

The secretary sighed doubtfully. "Colonel Barrabas, that's asking a lot. I'm supposed to be guarding his privacy, not, you know, letting people—"

"I understand your predicament, but this is fairly urgent. All I can do is ask you to trust me."

"Is it a matter of life or death?"

"Yes."

The ex-corporal considered a moment. Finally he spoke. "My ass is in your hands, Colonel Barrabas." He punched some instructions on the computer console at his side and stood up. "That releases the electronic locks. The files are in here."

He led the way into Jessup's inner office. A bank of metal cabinets stood shoulder to shoulder along one wall. The wide plate-glass window that normally overlooked the towers of Manhattan revealed a vortex of swirling snow that was the guts of a gathering blizzard.

"Nice day," the young man commented. He unhooked a clutch of keys from his belt and inserted a small circular key into a lock at the top of one of the cabinets. The top drawer opened, displaying a row of hanging files. Quickly he flipped through them. His fingers stopped.

"I have bad news," he said.

Barrabas looked over his shoulder.

"The file's empty." The assistant lifted the hanging file out of the drawer. Inside were several new-looking file folders, quite obviously containing nothing. "It's strange. I don't understand. This file was thick before he left a few days ago. I know because he wanted it on his desk every morning before he came in."

"And you have no idea what was in it?" Barrabas queried.

"Uh-uh. That's why he hired me. So I wouldn't look. I had a security clearance while I was in the army, you know."

The young man lifted the last file folder from the hanging file. A manila card slipped out and fluttered to the carpet. Barrabas leaned down, grabbed it and turned it over.

It was from the Banco Nacional de la República Boliviana, the main office in La Paz.

"A safety deposit box in the Plaza Murillo," Barrabas said, reading the Spanish. "Registered in the name of Walker Jessup."

"Is that helpful?" Ducett asked.

Barrabas shrugged. "It's as good a place as any to start."

A soft, persistent bell sounded in the outer office, and a look of alarm crossed the young man's face.

"The surveillance cameras. Someone's in the corridor." He went quickly back to his desk and deftly adjusted some switches to change the monitors.

Two men in dark coats emerged from the elevator and looked furtively about. As if by a prearranged plan, one disappeared through the emergency exit into the fire stairs. The other went back into the elevator. The doors closed, and once again the corridor was empty.

"The guy who went into the stairwell just made a big mistake. There's another stairwell on this side of the corridor. One of us can go upstairs, cross over and flush him out while the other one's waiting up here for him."

"Did Jessup tell you about this part of the job?" Barrabas asked.

In answer, Ducett opened the drawer of the desk and slipped out a small combat version of the Smith & Wesson M-39. He handled it as if it was an old friend.

"I won several awards for marksmanship in my company, sir."

"There's a small window in the fire door," Barrabas said. "The guy who went in there can't see us leave the office, but he can watch while I'm waiting for the elevator."

"I'll take care of him, Colonel."

"Let's try to keep at least one of these guys alive," Barrabas said. "I want to ask questions."

"I'll do my best, sir."

Barrabas and the young former soldier moved into the blind corridor that led from Jessup's office to the main hallway. In the hallway, Ducett slipped through a fire door into the second stairwell.

Barrabas reached inside his jacket and carefully removed his Browning HP. He kept his back to the wall as he slid along the corridor until he came to the fire door.

THE THREE MEN FROM INTERPOL raced across the plaza in pursuit of Nate Beck, unaware that Liam O'Toole was hightailing it after them. One slipped on the ice and fell. The other two kept going until they reached the railing that ran around the drive to the garage.

The third man picked himself up. He winced as he put his weight on one leg and limped several steps. Then he heard running footsteps crunching across the icy plaza.

Liam O'Toole bore down on him. The Interpol agent forgot about his sore leg. He ran for the parking garage, with O'Toole at his heels.

O'Toole grabbed the man by the collar of his jacket, ripping it down over his shoulder and twisting him around. He balled his fist and slugged it into the man's temple, dropping him like a stone.

Then the sound of gunfire broke through the wind, chilling O'Toole to the bone.

The Jaguar stopped, and the front door opened, slamming into Beck and blocking his progress to the fast-closing garage doors. The portly white-haired driver stepped out.

"Here now, young man," he scolded in a proper English accent. "You can't just go running in there, you know. That's a private parking garage."

Oh, Christ, thought Nate. A citizen trying to do his duty. "Please, mister, you don't understand." It was clear from the elderly gentleman's face that he wasn't going to try.

Nate hopped onto the Jaguar and slithered over the hood to the other side just as his pursuers reached the railing above.

The men from Interpol jumped, one at a time, to the driveway below. The Jaguar driver was incensed. His face turned bright red and he waved his arms.

"Here now! Who in hell do you think you are! You can't just go around—"

One of the men pulled a gun from underneath his coat and rammed it into the old man's guts. Two muffled shots knocked the irate fellow's remaining words right out of his mouth.

Interpol, like hell, thought Nate as he nosedived for the last few inches that were open below the swiftly closing door.

Too late.

He jerked his head and arms back before they were pinned between the door and the asphalt.

End of the line. Nate Beck crouched against the metal doors, his eyes flashing as he searched for an avenue of retreat. There was no place left to run.

"Stand up, Mr. Beck! Slowly!" one of his pursuers shouted. The man walked to the rear of the Jaguar. There was blood on the sleeve of his jacket, and a silencer had been added to the barrel of the gun. The second man stood by the open door of the Jaguar, waiting. At his feet, the body of the elderly driver bled into the snow-covered asphalt.

The first assassin aimed at Beck, using both hands to brace for the shot.

Suddenly he flew forward as something walloped him from behind. A brief sunburst of blood and bone exploded from the back of his head. The man tipped forward, fell over the hood of the Jaguar, slid quickly to the pavement and flipped onto his back.

The second man looked up at the railing, whipping his gun around to pull the trigger at Nate's unexpected defender.

Liam O'Toole pulled first.

The bullet tore into the man's forehead, throwing him against the car. Falling slowly, his knees buckling, he landed on the front seat of the Jaguar and collapsed inside, his legs strewn awkwardly out the open door.

Nate rose to his feet.

O'Toole leaped down to the driveway.

"You okay?" He bent to examine the body in the Jaguar, quickly rifling the pockets of the coats.

"Sùre, I'm okay." Nate looked around for his hat. The wind had blown it into the corner near the doors. "They said they were from Interpol."

"Interpol, hell," O'Toole muttered. He moved to the second one and found the billfold with the identification inside it. It was a small two-bit piece of cardboard, readily available in the joke shops on Forty-second Street. From the distance it did the trick. But it wasn't Interpol. There were no other pieces of ID.

"Looks like someone's trying awful hard to be our buddies," O'Toole speculated, finishing his search and standing.

"Either that or Beverley," Nate said. He approached the red-haired Irishman. "Thanks, Liam."

"It's okay, Nate. As long as they keep missing."

BARRABAS WAITED, keeping one eye on the entrance to the stairwell and the other on the elevator. There was a gunman behind each door, both waiting for him to leave Jessup's office and push for the elevator.

Before long he heard the click of the door handle, and the door to the stairwell opened. He heard Ducett's voice.

"Now leave the gun right there on the floor and just keep those hands high and wide, mister. Walk real nice and slow into the hall—"

The medium-tall man with the long dark coat moved through the doorway. Suddenly he kicked back, shoving the door into Ducett's face and knocking the young man backward.

The gun man failed to see Barrabas as he ran to the elevator and pressed the button.

Barrabas was right behind him.

He jumped behind the gunman and slammed him into the elevator door with his Browning pressed into his back. "Now you just tell your buddy in there to drop his gun and come quietly," the colonel instructed between gritted teeth.

The elevator doors opened. This time there were two passengers. The gunman and his square ugly Ingram submachine gun.

His eyes locked with Barrabas's over his buddy's shoulder.

The buddy threw his hands up. "Don't sho—"

The gunman in the elevator shot.

Barrabas threw his captive forward and swung to the side. The man caught the submachine gun fire in a bloody line across his torso. He screamed and fell on top of the gunman, and the submachine gun clattered on the floor as the doors began to slide closed.

Barrabas jumped forward and grabbed a handful of the surprised gunman's hair, pulling him forward. The doors closed on the man's head. He screamed and flailed at the doors as they released and slid open.

Barrabas yanked the man forward from the elevator into the hall, driving him headfirst into the opposite wall. The gunman crumpled, semiconscious, to the floor.

Jimmy Ducett emerged from the stairwell and watched in astonishment.

Barrabas reached down, grabbed the man's hair again and pulled his head up. He slammed the barrel of his Browning into the gunman's neck.

"I want some answers. Like who sent you. Now!" he shouted angrily.

The man looked up at Barrabas and almost smiled. He bit down hard on the back of his jaw before answering defiantly. "You'll never—"

Suddenly the man stiffened, and his eyes jutted horribly from their sockets. Spittle drooled from his mouth and ran down his chin.

"Shit," Barrabas cursed, stepping back and putting the Browning away.

"What in hell killed him?" Ducett asked, incredulous.

Barrabas knelt by the dead man and carefully used both hands to open the his mouth. Resting on the corpse's tongue was the small, perfect cap from the top of a tooth.

"Cyanide."

"Whew. That's heavy going." Jimmy Ducett shook his head in disbelief. "Who the fuck are you dealing with, anyway?"

Barrabas stood up slowly. "Whoever it is, the answer isn't here."

"It's in Bolivia?"

Barrabas nodded. "In Bolivia—with Walker Jessup."

NANOS WATCHED THE SMOKE CURL AWAY from the smoking ruins on the hillside and thought about the breakfast that had been consumed by the explosion. Nearby Claude and Billy Two negotiated on the telephone in the booth in the village square. Nanos rubbed his shoulder. Starfoot had hit him so hard he was going to have bruises for a week. It had been so long now since he'd eaten he thought he was going to pass out under the hot Central American sun. Life was a real bitch. All because of the former Miss Uruguay.

Claude Hayes and Billy Two left the phone booth and walked toward Nanos.

"Hey, guys, how 'bout it? Can we eat?" Nanos implored. "Refried beans. Defried beans. Freeze-dried beans. I don't care. Anything. Food! Sustenance!"

Hayes shook his head as they approached. "You'll have to hold on a little longer, Alex. We got a plane to catch."

"A plane to—"

"And if we leave now, we'll barely make it to the airfield in time. It's three hours away."

"B-b-but...did you talk to the colonel? Or Jessup?"

Billy Two shook his head. "Uh-uh. To Jessup's secretary. We just missed the colonel, but he left a message."

"An urgent message," Hayes added.

Nanos looked from Hayes to Starfoot.

"Please," he said wearily. "Tell me."

"He wants us to get there as fast as we can," Billy told him.

"That was the message," Hayes confirmed. "Meet me in La Paz."

BARRABAS WAITED NEAR THE EXIT DOOR on the sixth level of the open parking garage, watching the blizzard gather force and sweep through the streets outside. He kept the collar of his sheepskin jacket pulled up high and retreated to a corner where he was protected from the strong icy wind but also had a view of the ramp.

His hand in his pocket gripped the butt of the Browning. He was alert, ready to act, and aware that danger might come any moment from any direction.

Especially if he had been lured into a trap.

He heard the latch on the exit door turn, and the door opened outward. He pressed against the cement wall behind it. A woman stepped through.

Miss Roseline wore one of those long quilted winter coats, tied at the waist, and with the hood pulled up tightly around her head. She looked carefully around the parking level as she stepped through, missing Barrabas until after the door closed behind her.

When she saw him, she jumped halfway out of her skin, her voice frozen in her throat.

Barrabas watched her without speaking.

"Y-you're Barrabas?" she asked tentatively. She was chewing gum. "I'm a little late. I'm sorry. I had to drive from Washington in this storm. I parked on the third level and walked up so no one would see us. You frightened the living daylights out of me."

The colonel remained silent.

"I guess I recognized you from your hair. Not many men as young as you have white hair," she stammered nervously, pulling off her gloves. Her long nails were painted with bright red polish. She delicately plucked the little ball of gum from her mouth and flicked it away.

"I've never done this before." For a moment she wrestled with her purse, pulling out a cigarette. She tried to light it with a disposable lighter, but the circulating wind kept blowing the flame out.

His suspicions ninety percent quelled, Barrabas took the lighter from her and cupped it in his hand. He lit her cigarette.

"Thank you," she said, blowing out smoke as if it were a sigh of relief. She was a pretty woman, although perhaps a little too heavily made-up.

"You're nervous," Barrabas said.

"Like I said, I've never been a whistle blower." She breathed heavily, uncertain of how to continue.

"I work in the office of a senator. Yesterday evening I overheard a conversation about you.... I thought you should know about it."

Barrabas listened carefully but continued to say nothing. It was a basic trick he'd learned while doing intelligence work in the army. Silence made the informer uncomfortable. In their effort to fill it up, they blabbed away, and the chatter was a useful gauge of their seriousness.

The woman gave a little laugh to conceal her nervousness. "I guess this makes me Deep Throat. You know, like in the Watergate scandal."

"Is that why you chose a parking garage?"

She looked surprised. "I don't know. I guess so. I never thought of it really.

"What did you want to tell me?"

"You have to promise me never to breathe a word, to say nothing, ever. I don't know what they'd do to me if they found out. Some of the men he knows are ruthless."

"It's a little late now to decide you don't trust me."

The woman shivered and puffed anxiously on the cigarette. "Yeah. I guess so." She bit her lip. "If anyone asks, just say a little bird told you."

Barrabas couldn't help smiling at her. "Promise."

Miss Roseline looked visibly relieved.

"Now tell me what happened," Barrabas said.

"The senator has a friend or colleague, a man who comes every now and then. I don't even know who he is. His name's never marked in the appointment book. Sometimes he just shows up. Other times the senator tells me he's expecting someone, but never says who. The senator always sees him, no matter how unexpectedly he drops in. So yesterday I listened..."

She stopped for a moment and seemed embarrassed. Barrabas waited patiently for her to continue.

"It's the first time I've ever done that. I don't know why. I just had this feeling. But this is what I heard. They talked about you and Walker Jessup. They want you killed. You and all your people. There's something going on in Bolivia with a group called the Black International."

Barrabas looked at her blankly.

"You don't seem surprised."

"A lot of people are trying to kill me, miss. So far none of them have succeeded. In a minute I want you to start at the beginning. But what did they say about the Fixer?"

"Walker Jessup? Forget about him."

"Why?"

"It's too late. He's already dead."

9

High in the Andes, the snow-covered peak of Illimani towered above the smaller mountains surrounding the Institute of Linguistic Semantics. The collection of low one-story buildings almost filled a narrow treeless plateau, which pointed like a finger to heaven. At thirty-seven hundred meters above sea level, heaven was not too far away.

There was no fence or barrier surrounding the Institute, which appeared to be an offering on the Andean altar to the golden sun. A carpet of grass ran to the edge of the plateau where rocky precipices dropped several hundred meters before breaking in a valley of stones.

The Institute of Linguistic Semantics was, semantically speaking, a language school. Language was taught there—particularly German—among a wider range of subjects dealing with culture, history and ideology. Extracurricular activity included sports, with an emphasis on modern warfare.

A narrow road carved into the rock wound steeply up one side of the plateau and ran like a gash of brown across the green grass to the collection of several dozen buildings. Not far from the top, a small convoy of vehicles struggled uphill, the compression in the engines low in the high altitude. There were two cars—a black limousine in front and a Ford behind. In the middle was an old four-by-four van that might once have served as an armored vehicle to carry cash for Brinks or Wells Fargo.

In the back of the limousine, Adolf von Rausch eyed the interior of the compound. In an open quadrant surrounded by the low barrackslike wood buildings, several hundred young men were vigorously engaged in calisthenics.

"The Fiancés of Death," von Rausch snorted. He rode alone in the back compartment. "At least Barbier could have been imaginative. Instead, he is merely vulgar."

His driver stopped in front of a long building. Three large wings, which housed lecture theaters, sprouted along the back. He opened his boss's door and stood back.

It was summer in the southern hemisphere, but high in the Andes, early in the morning, the temperature was almost down to freezing. Von Rausch strode briskly from the car, sniffing the fresh mountain air and surveying the surrounding mountain peaks.

His silvery yellow hair was long on top, oiled and combed straight back. He was a tall man and stood erect. He wore a expensive dark blue wool coat and walked with a steady military gait.

The uniform was different, he reflected, as the van and the Ford pulled to a stop behind the limousine, but he felt almost as good today as he had on those wonderful mornings forty-five years earlier when he had been master of half of Europe.

A short muscular Hispanic with scars on his cheeks emerged from the front seat of the Ford.

"Señor Rausch," he called over the roof of the car, barely moving his mouth as he spoke.

The silver-haired man turned.

"The prisoners." The Hispanic jerked his head toward the back seat of the Ford.

"Guard them, Joaquin," von Rausch said as he turned and walked up the steps into the building. A young man in a dark green uniform sat at a desk in the reception area. He rose and snapped to attention as von Rausch entered.

"I want to see Señor Barbier," he said, slipping off his gloves. "Immediately."

"Señor Barbier is giving a lecture to the generals. He asked that you join them on your arrival."

"Which theater?"

The soldier led him a short distance down a corridor to some double doors that stood closed beneath a glowing red light bulb. He opened one of them, and von Rausch quietly slipped into the hushed and somber darkness.

The hall was lit by a bank of candles on either side of the podium at the front. Karl Barbier, Director of the Institute, was giving a lecture. His most exclusive audience, fourteen generals, sat stiff and upright in their chairs, raptly attentive. Rows of medals on their chests and hats were burnished by the soft glow of the candlelight.

"Remember!" Barbier exhorted, balling his fist and striding across the front of the room. He was short and bald, and whatever military bearing he may once have had, had long ago capitulated to the spread of middle age.

"Remember! The people are worms. They slink to the ground and crawl on their soft white bellies in the earth when confronted by intractable force. Power must be unyielding. The will to act must show no mercy."

He stopped and glared at the row of generals who watched, enraptured by his words and his theatrics. He took a deep lungful of air and raised his arms.

"This is the face, the only face, we will show the people." His voice lowered, grew tender, almost fatherly and affectionate. "This is the face of National Socialism!" he ended on a whisper.

The generals burst into appreciative applause, led by a beaming man with a long nose and a wide forehead in the middle of the first row. This one turned slightly in his chair as he clapped his hands, acknowledging the applause of the others as if it were for him.

Von Rausch stood at the back of the hall and received silently the brief acknowledgment of his presence when Barbier's eyes met his. He nodded and gave a slight bow.

"Gentlemen, Saviors of Bolivia!" Barbier exhorted, "Let us rise and sing the national anthem of our beloved patrimony."

In unison the generals stood and began to sing: *"Bolivianos, el hado propicio corono nuestros votos anhelo..."* (Bolivians, propitious fate has crowned our hopes). The fervor of their patriotism rang in their words, and their voices rose to heaven like righteousness melting on the tongue of an eagle.

It was an old familiar scene to von Rausch, a man who, in his seventy years, had seen much. The enthusiastic voices of the earnest generals, and the sight of the great red flag with its black swastika behind the podium, brought tears to his eyes. Once again the sensation of terrible loss came to him, and he mourned.

The voices of the generals faded to a close on the last notes of the magnificent anthem. They stood, shuffling with slight discomfort, as if they wondered what to do next.

"Gentlemen," Barbier called to them, his voice warmer and less formal. "Let us retire to the lounge for coffee. Tomorrow is an important day for us, and for the nation. We can relax and discuss a few of the final details of the coup d'état."

The Bolivian generals readily agreed. As they filed out a side door, Karl Barbier made his way to the back of the lecture room and approached von Rausch. "Welcome to the Institute, Adolf," he said. "Did you bring it?"

"It's out front, Karl Barbier." Von Rausch's manner of speaking had a unintentional arrogance to it, in part deriving from the blue-blooded Prussian family he had grown up in.

Although he was aware that such distinctions were, under the doctrines of National Socialism, irrelevant, he was unable to feel completely free of condescension toward Barbier. After all, von Rausch had been a war hero, and later a leading general of the SS.

Barbier had merely been the head of the Gestapo in a large administrative city in one of the occupied territories. His work had nevertheless been important—his chief claim to fame being the elimination of the leader of the resistance in the country in question—but it had lacked the privilege and the simple elegance of the methods used by Hitler's elite armed guard.

The two men had come together in the late 1940s in an Italian monastery that had acted as a way station for diehard Nazis on their way to South America. Both had performed certain valuable services for the OSS—the American military intelligence organization—after the war. In return the Allied armies of the occupation had turned a blind eye to the underground railroad that had supplied passports, identities and transportation to the southern hemisphere.

They and other like-minded fellow Nazis who had been thrown together in the flight to safety had become the nucleus of the Kameradenwerk. Like the ODESSA, it was a fraternal order working toward the mutual security and welfare of those who had once served the Third Reich.

Escape, secrecy and the danger of Israeli agents had brought them together, but the caste divisions that had governed their respective positions in Europe continued to exist as their lives took shape in South America.

Von Rausch currently worked as a highly paid and well-respected security consultant for the vicious, repressive military dictatorship in Chile. After the junta in that country had seized power, his expertise as a former member of the SS in building concentration camps had been invaluable.

Barbier had lived in retirement for many years. Eventually, as the network of Nazis had made contacts with like-minded nationals of their adopted countries—Uruguay, Argentina, Chile, Paraguay— an idea had grown into a plan. Bolivia was the key to its success. Barbier's unwaning devotion to the cause of National Socialism had earned him the position of central coordinator—Director of the Institute of Linguistic Semantics.

Despite these differences in background, von Rausch was aware of some other difference between them, something that eluded him. Over and over again he had asked himself what it was, and always the answer remained just beyond reach.

Barbier cleared his throat. "Perhaps you will join the generals at coffee," he invited. "I would like to see your famous invention. I've waited forty-one years for this opportunity."

"There is another matter, somewhat more urgent. The favor our friends in Washington asked us to perform in exchange for certain...indulgences. We may not have been successful. It's a matter of some concern."

Barbier shifted uncomfortably at the unpleasant news. He reached two fingers into the breast pocket of his white shirt and withdrew a small silver vial with a tiny spoon hanging from the neck by a thin chain.

"We'll discuss this," Barbier said, unscrewing the lid and inserting the spoon into the vial. He withdrew a tiny quantity of crystalline white powder and lifted it to his nose. After one quick snort, he repeated the procedure for the other nostril. He sniffled several times as he waited for the almost instantaneous effects of the drug.

Von Rausch waited and watched, unimpressed by Barbier's addiction to cocaine. Finally Barbier continued.

"Our American allies have been of much help, and they won't be pleased if the Black International doesn't carry out its end of the bargain. But I must put in an appearance with our generals and answer questions for them first. Please, join us."

"Certainly," von Rausch answered quickly, eager for the opportunity to meet the military men who had joined their efforts. "Are they ready?"

"Yes, I think so," Barbier replied. The two men walked around the seats in the auditorium to the side exit. "Their ideology is still...how shall I say... weak."

"You mean they aren't particularly intelligent? We had that problem with our friends in many of the occupied countries."

"And how did you deal with it?"

"These are men of action, not men of words or thought. If they're ruthless, intelligence isn't important."

"Hmmm, ruthless," Barbier reflected. "They're ruthless, I suppose, although I can't be certain if it's because they believe in our cause, or if they're merely greedy."

"Greedy?"

"Their reward...they show particular interest in that. We're giving up a great deal."

Von Rausch shrugged. "Not really. We've promised them a monopoly on the profits from the co-caine industry, which, heretofore, we've controlled.

We will, however, continue to have our own 'service' charges.''

"And the revenues we've been using to finance our military activities will be replaced by direct subsidies from the Bolivian state.''

"Exactly,'' von Rausch said. "That is the plan— to create a Nazi axis through the southern half of South America. Chile, Uruguay, now Bolivia, and someday, Argentina, once again.''

"Then the Kameradenwerk will do its work from a position of authority, power and invincibility.''

"Yes. As for greed, you must be aware that it's an excellent motivating factor. These are Hispanic generals we're dealing with, not Aryans. They're effective, but they don't hold ideals as lofty as we. They're a little vulgar, a little bit like children. And so we put before them the prospect of immense fortunes, as one dangles candy before a baby.''

"You're skilled in these delicate manipulations, Adolf,'' Barbier said, smiling as they reached the door to the lounge. "I was always more direct in my methods of persuasion.''

"Yes, I know.'' For a moment von Rausch had a glimpse of the real difference between Barbier and him.

Barbier pushed the door open, and the two men entered the lounge. The generals chatted together in small clusters of three or four, holding coffee cups and cigarettes. They greeted the director and his well-known guest with enthusiasm and a smattering of polite applause.

For the next half hour, von Rausch politely made his rounds, with a smile and a word of praise for each of the fourteen medal-decked generals. Finally he was left alone with General Garcia Cheza, the man with the long nose and the broad, unlined forehead.

"You must be very excited, General Cheza," von Rausch commented. "Tomorrow you'll become the president of the República Boliviana."

"I assure you, the coup d'état will be a complete and total success." Cheza sniffled several times and spoke slowly, as if he was choosing each word with the utmost care. "Of course, there can be no question of it."

"Of course." Privately von Rausch entertained his own secret thoughts about General Garcia Cheza. The man was useful because he had a particular penchant for stupidity. He did as he was told, too unimaginative to take any initiatives of his own; for those reasons he was exceptionally useful.

"There is one question, though, of course." Cheza furrowed his brow as if he earnestly contemplated a serious problem.

Von Rausch merely stared at him.

"The profits from the cocaine industry that your people currently control—"

"Ah, that," the former SS general replied.

"Yes, these profits will come to us, to my colleagues and me entirely?"

"Absolutely, my friend. You seem troubled. There's no need to be. Our people control the cultivation and processing of thousands of kilos of cocaine each year, as well as the network of importers who arrange for shipment to the United States and Europe. You'll control that monopoly as of tomorrow."

General Cheza shook his head slowly as he absorbed von Rausch's assurances.

"Gracias. This is important," he said. "I speak for my colleagues when I say you are most welcome as our ally, Señor Rausch. And I hope we will be able to use your expertise in our government as our comrades in Chile do."

Von Rausch saw an opportunity to approach a delicate subject that had been on his mind for some time.

"I'm sure that will be the case, Generalissimo Cheza. You will obviously have to deal with the opposition efficiently. Señor Barbier and I have, in fact, prepared a list of a hundred and eight-five names—"

He was interrupted when a much-decorated general, elderly and walking with the assistance of a cane, approached. Cheza bent to listen to the shriveled old man.

"You have asked him, Generalissimo?" the old general queried the leader of the imminent coup.

"*Sí*, General Cabeza. He assures us all the profits will be ours."

Cheza straightened and beamed at von Rausch, a trifle embarrassed. "We were discussing the matter earlier."

Cabeza tapped Cheza on the arm, and once again the generalissimo leaned down to listen.

"How much?" the old man asked.

"Ha, ha," Cheza laughed, slightly nervous. He straightened and looked at von Rausch.

"Approximately one hundred million dollars a year," the German answered, annoyed at both the interruption and its trivial nature. "Now about this list of a hundred and eight-five names, Generalissimo Cheza. These are potential troublemakers for your regime and are best eliminated."

Again the elderly general pulled on Cheza's sleeve, motioning him aside for a private conversation.

"Excuse me, please." The generalissimo smiled graciously.

"Certainly," von Rausch said stiffly, stepping back as the two Bolivian generals moved away in earnest conversation.

"How goes it?" a voice asked. Karl Barbier had moved behind him.

"They seem much more interested in the profits from the cocaine monopoly than in the real purpose of the takeover of the Bolivian government," von Rausch replied. "Perhaps we should call them the cocaine generals."

"Patience, Adolf. You yourself have just said that these are Hispanics, not Aryans."

"Yes. I suppose they can't be expected to share the same nobility of purpose."

"Yet I assure you, my own legion of elite soldiers, the Fiancés of Death, do. And tomorrow, when they march through the streets of La Paz, it will be evident. Now, Adolf, let us go away from all this. I'm interested in your famous invention. And you spoke of a troubling matter. Shall we leave, quietly?"

Barbier and von Rausch slipped through the doors into the reception area and quickly made their way to the quadrant outside. The sun was higher, burning the remaining night moisture from the dry mountain air. The young men in the quadrant continued their exercises. The heavy old van was still parked in front of the building. Several of the former SS general's Chilean myrmidons lounged against the black Ford.

"I love this location," Barbier reflected, surveying the mountain peaks surrounding the plateau.

"It is as if you were nestled in the palm of God's outstretched hand," von Rausch said.

"The buildings with the chimneys, on the other side of the exercise field, are the birthplace of our little enterprise. Without the profits of the cocaine industry, we could never have financed our operations." Barbier pointed for Rausch's benefit. "They contain the factory in which cocoa leaves are refined into a sticky white paste called cocaine sulphate."

"And what is in those barrels stockpiled over there?" von Rausch asked, pointed to several hundred forty-five-gallon oil drums near the drug factory.

"Chemicals. Ether and acetone used to turn the paste into cocaine hydrochloride—the powder most people associate with the drug. Very dangerous, highly volatile liquids. We're phasing them out. It's much easier to smuggle the paste into America anyway."

"And now this entire plant will go to the generals," von Rausch said, somewhat regretfully.

"Not entirely." Barbier smiled. "We've made arrangements to maintain a private income from the drug trade—although the generals believe they are receiving a monopoly. We don't want to burn our bridges, do we? Now, where is the famous invention?"

Von Rausch gestured toward the van.

Barbier conducted an examination, then said, "Brilliant. One would never know."

"I shall never forget the day when the first of these went into operation. It was July, 1940, in one of the Baltic republics. Field Marshal Göring himself came to watch the demonstration. And later, *der Führer* awarded me—"

"You mentioned another problem," Barbier interrupted.

The older white-haired Nazi stiffened. He didn't abide interruptions, and this was the second one in less than an hour. He considered a reprimand, but stopped himself in the interest of compatibility. Nothing was more important than the success of the current project—not even the insult that he sustained from a lackey like Karl Barbier.

Von Rausch turned to his aides. "Bring the prisoners out of the car!" he ordered.

The men leaning against the Ford spun into action. They quickly dragged two men, their wrists and ankles shackled, from the back of the car. The prisoners looked morose but defiant.

"These men reported to me from Geneva," von Rausch explained as he and Barbier walked closer to the prisoners. "They were entrusted—along with several of our European agents—with the responsibility of eliminating this Barrabas. Not only did they fail to eliminate this man that our American friends desperately want out of the way, but three of our European agents were killed in the action. Our friends in the Fatherland are not happy about that."

The prisoners listened intently to von Rausch's words, scarcely bothering to conceal their resentment. One of them suddenly spoke up.

"You were not there, Señor Rausch, so you did not see this man. He drove like a devil. We would have needed an army to—"

"Silence!" von Rausch commanded. His lip curled in anger, and he almost raised his hand to strike the man. "I'm not interested in excuses. I'm interested only in results."

He turned to Barbier.

"Come." The two men walked out of hearing distance of the men near the Ford.

"And the agents in New York, Montreal, Acapulco and Belize?" Barbier asked quietly.

"The former Miss Uruguay was unsuccessful also. She, however, is beyond retribution. We haven't received the reports of the others yet."

"We went to so much work to obtain the information leading to the whereabouts of this secret commando team. I hope we haven't made a mistake."

"You're afraid of these commandos coming here? It's impossible. Dead men don't tell tales, and either they're dead or our agents are dead."

"I agree that it's unlikely. No, I'm afraid that our American friends won't be pleased by our failure, and their assistance in Washington to calm any fears regarding the new regime that will take over in Bolivia tomorrow are important—invaluable, actually."

"I've used only the best agents," von Rausch said. "And all the resources of the Chilean secret police and their worldwide links to our European brethren. Still, we can't tolerate failure. These two—" he gestured with a toss of his head toward the prisoners "—have set a bad example."

"And so we must make a good example out of them." Barbier's suggestion was accompanied by a smile.

"I agree," von Rausch added, shivering with anticipation. "Except for these eliminations, everything has gone so well. I feel optimistic, Karl. Better than I have ever felt since the vicious betrayal of the German people forty years ago. Better even than when our people seized power in Chile in 1973."

"It's time to take off our gloves and show that we're ruthless," Barbier said firmly. "Is the van in working order?"

"I guarantee it," von Rausch said. "However, it hasn't been tested, and what better opportunity to show the generals—"

"Yes, the generals. They're sincere, and yet I fear they don't fully understand what I mean when I use the word 'ruthless.' Now is our opportunity to graphically illustrate it."

"Excellent," von Rausch concluded. "Send for them."

Barbier returned to the building while the former SS general ordered one of his men to start the van and idle the engine. The rear doors were flung open, revealing a shiny stainless-steel interior devoid of any openings save for vents set along the walls near the floor. A thick rubber gasket surrounded the rear doors, providing an airtight seal.

A few moments later Barbier emerged from the building with the cocaine generals in tow.

"Put the prisoners inside," von Rausch ordered. The two men in shackles shouted and began to struggle. Their resistance was of no use. They were quickly overpowered and thrown into the rear compartment of the van. The doors were slammed shut and a wheel was turned to seal the van completely.

Feeling buoyant and pleased, Adolf von Rausch went to the back of the van and peered through the thick wire-reinforced glass window in the door.

One of the prisoners gave him the finger.

Von Rausch smiled, unperturbed.

He stepped aside, noting the exhaust fumes pouring from the tail pipe. He walked around the van and stood near the driver's cab. His hand rested on a lever that protruded from the undercarriage. Quietly he addressed the generals.

"The principle is simple, gentlemen, and highly efficient. I simply pull this lever here..."

He carried out his instructions as he lectured.

"And the carbon monoxide from the engine exhaust is immediately recirculated into a ventilation system that feeds it into the compartment. The gas is deadly. The van need only drive a few kilometers—three times around the compound, for example, or the distance from the prison to the burial ground—and the occupants of the compartment will be dead."

There was a murmur of approval from the coterie of Bolivian generals. Adolf Rausch, decorated inventor of the mobile gas chamber, had impressed the military elite once again.

"You may observe for yourself," von Rausch invited them, gesturing to the windows at the back of the van, "as Field Marshal Göring once did in Riga when my invention was first unveiled."

The curious generals surged forward and peered through the thick glass windows. The two prisoners yelled and made obscene gestures. The generals laughed. They could hear nothing.

One of the men inside began to cough slightly. They looked at each other with expressions of alarm. It seemed they were arguing. One of them got down on his knees and sniffed at the vents that ran along the floor. He got up and shook his head at the other one.

"Of course he can smell nothing," von Rausch explained. "Carbon monoxide is an odorless gas. They will simply fall asleep, painlessly, oblivious even to their own death."

Von Rausch quietly stepped aside as the fourteen generals jockeyed to look.

Fifteen minutes later the old Nazi ordered the engine shut off. Fans were switched on to pipe the carbon monoxide from the gas chamber. With quiet dignity, von Rausch moved to the back of the van.

"Now, generals. A vivid illustration of the effectiveness of this method."

The clouds that had been snagged by Mount Illimani's peak abruptly broke away, and a shaft of heavy sunlight burst from the heavens to shine on the grassy plateau. Von Rausch spun the wheel on the back doors and proudly swung them open. The bodies of the two prisoners flopped forward in a heap over the tailgate of the van.

"The...ahem...merchandise in the van tends to move toward the rear doors as the chamber fills with gas. This also makes the unloading much simpler."

The generals burst into appreciative applause. Barbier moved in beside von Rausch to look. The two dead men looked as if they merely slept.

"It does lack the personal touch," Barbier commented with a hint of arrogance.

Suddenly von Rausch realized what it was about Barbier that disturbed him. Killing, death, executions—it was a messy business, however one looked at it. He had set himself the goal of making it as refined, as delicate, as polite as possible. The mobile gas chamber was, to his mind, the pinnacle of this endeavor. Barbier had always liked to use his bare hands. The difference between the two men could be easily summed up—one was civilized, and one was savage. The former SS general had never had any doubt that the Gestapo could learn from his methods.

Karl Barbier spoke, breaking into von Rausch's thoughts.

"Now that the generals have seen that your method of execution is clean, simple, cheap and painless, they'll be more prepared to follow our suggestions regarding the elimination of opposition. You do have a list prepared, don't you?"

"Yes. It was prepared with the assistance of the secret police in Santiago. There are a hundred and eighty-five Bolivians on it—opposition leaders, unionists, professors. To destroy opposition, cut off its head. To cut off its head, liquidate the leaders."

"That truly is the meaning of National Socialism," Barbier concluded. "Tell me," he added with a little laugh, "how fast does the mobile gas chamber work on a big fat American?"

Adolf von Rausch shared Barbier's amusement. "You mean this Walker Jessup? The size of the person to be eliminated makes little difference to the amount of air consumed by the average pair of adult lungs. Has his usefulness ended?"

"I believe so," Barbier answered. "He's told us where to find Barrabas and his team of commandos."

"Karl, please," von Rausch said graciously. "Be my guest."

Barbier gave a curt nod and said, "In time, we must, of course, inform our American friends that we have thus far failed to eliminate these commandos. But I hope, quite frankly, that we have heard the last of them."

"If not, Karl, we can simply invite them here and take them for a ride."

The Nazis laughed long and hard at their private joke.

10

Barrabas woke at 6:00 a.m. in a room in the old Concord hotel in La Paz. His eyes opened to a view of an ornate ceiling high overhead. He quickly rolled out of bed and put on his work clothes—wool slacks and a casual blue shirt. Thin shafts of yellow light cut through the seams of the curtains over the double windows. He unlatched the louvered balcony doors and threw them open.

In the distance the snow-dappled peak of Illimani caught the first rays of the sun. Two stories below, the Plaza Murillo was wide and silent and virtually empty. A flock of dirty pigeons hovered around the statue of Simón Bolívar, and an old Indian woman wearing a felt hat wandered around the base of the monument, feeding them handfuls of corn from a woven sack.

Barrabas sniffed at the crisp air of the high Andes. The lack of oxygen made a palpable difference in the texture of the air. For the natives of the highest capital city in the world, it wasn't a problem. But it took time for the human body to adjust to life at an altitude of thirty-seven hundred meters.

Barrabas knew that he and his soldiers would tire more easily up here, and weariness was a liability in the kind of hard, fast moving strikes that spelled success or failure for a commando team. But there were other problems to think about. How to obtain munitions and ordnance. And how to get into Jessup's safety deposit box in a Bolivian bank. Geoff Bishop and Claude Hayes had been sent to Lima with instructions to find a helicopter and go to Arequipa, a Peruvian city a hundred and fifty miles from the Bolivian capital. The rest of the mercs had arrived as tourists and checked into the Concord late the night before. It might take days to do the proper surveillance and set up a heist. And he still hadn't told the mercs about his secret rendezvous with the senator's secretary the day before.

The city was quiet but quick to awaken. A car shot around the plaza and disappeared behind the presidential palace. A half-ton pulled up in front of the National Congress. Armed soldiers carefully exited from the back and smoothed their uniforms before replacing the guards at the gate.

Directly across the square from the hotel stood the target—the Banco Nacional de la República Boliviana.

As Barrabas watched, a caretaker stepped up to the bronze front doors of the domed nineteenth-century Spanish colonial building. He selected a key from among many on an iron ring and inserted it into the old-fashioned lock. The three-meter-high doors swung smoothly back like the well-oiled gates of a fortress, and were fastened by hooks to the wall. Then the caretaker pulled a rag from his pocket and began to polish the wrought-iron grille that covered the thick glass on the inner doors.

Introductory bank-robbing, Barrabas mused.

There was a knock on the door, and Barrabas crossed the room and opened it. O'Toole gave him a curt nod and slipped inside.

"Top o' the mornin' to you, Colonel," he said, deliberately using the inflection of his native brogue.

"Come here, Liam." Barrabas waved him to the window and pointed across the Plaza Murillo. "There it is."

As Barrabas and O'Toole watched, a shiny black Mercedes limousine pulled up in front of the bank, and the chauffeur held the door open for a white-haired man in an expensive suit who carried a black briefcase. A middle-aged woman in a dark dress emerged from the front of the limo and accompanied him through the great front doors to the interior of the bank.

"The head honcho arrives early," O'Toole commented. "Colonel, you really figure Walker Jessup is out there somewhere?"

"Liam, Bolivia has just about everything you could ask for. A lot of poor Indians and a few rich people who run the show. The current president is a nice old guy whose government borrows billions of dollars from American banks just to stay afloat. Meanwhile, the entire economy is really based on the illicit cocaine industry. And ambitious generals are chafing at the bit. This is exactly the kind of place the Fixer does his dirty work. The place is ripe.''

"Ripe for what?"

Barrabas didn't answer. He had his eyes on something else.

Squadrons of army helicopters were flying in formation through the gaps between the snow-tipped mountains around La Paz. At the same time the faraway rumble of heavy trucks thundered ominously across the city. The long avenues that led from the distant foothills to the Plaza Murillo filled rapidly with military convoys.

The hotel shook with the growling roar of tanks rolling into the square and taking up positions outside the presidential palace and the National Congress.

On the farthest horizon of the thin blue sky, two pinpoints of black quickly transformed into small strategic fighters, the used surplus of some NATO country.

"A coup d'état," Barrabas said. Miss Roseline's information was accurate. So far.

O'Toole was stunned. "Your timing is right on, that's for sure," he said.

At the Banco Nacional, the little old caretaker scurried outside and quickly began to pull the big front doors shut.

Barrabas nudged O'Toole. "Who speaks Spanish?"

"You. Hatton. Billy Two, but most of the time he's strictly looney tunes."

"He could pass, though. Because I just figured out how we're going to do it."

"What do you mean?"

"Rob the national bank. Look there."

O'Toole stuck his head farther out the window just in time to see a line of armored personnel carriers as they poured into the Plaza Murillo.

"You mean just go in through the front doors?" O'Toole asked.

"That's what I mean. We need uniforms, guns and an armored truck—and it's all right down there for the taking. Liam, right now we're looking at our very own Christmas tree."

At that moment there was an urgent knock on the door. Barrabas left the window to answer it. A short excited man whose plump belly protruded through the open jacket of his suit bowed deferentially.

"Excuse me, I'm the hotel manager. We're having some difficulties in the capital as you may have noticed—"

From the window came two loud explosions, followed by the chatter of rifle fire. The old hotel trembled, and the manager clutched the door frame.

"Those two fighters just blew the front off the presidential palace," O'Toole shouted from the window.

The little man at the door pushed into the room, flapping his hands. He rushed across the room and shut the louvered doors.

"No, no, *señores*. You must not be looking outside. I assure you, the problem is only temporary. If, please, you will to stay in your room, we will endeavor to make you as comfortable as possible."

O'Toole ignored the fat man and opened the doors again. The columns that had, a minute earlier, held up the three-story portico over the front of the executive mansion had been reduced to rubble. Smoke poured from the second-story windows of the palace. Soldiers leapt from the personnel carriers and began to attack the guards outside the palace gates. Three more personnel carriers stopped outside the hotel, and uniformed men rushed to set up machine guns and pile sandbags along the facade of the elegant old building. More men ran inside the building.

Resistance looked fierce as soldiers took up positions outside the National Congress buildings on the opposite side of the Plaza Murillo. Tanks swiveled, aiming their guns at the front doors of the Congress. It was impossible to tell who was on what side.

The coup was obviously extremely well planned. It hit the capital like a lightning bolt.

The hotel manager flitted back to the door and shook his finger at them. "*Señores*, remember. Stay away from the windows. Is very dangerous. And, please, you must also stay in your room until further notification."

Barrabas peered into the long wide hallway as he closed the door behind the little man. Armed soldiers were taking up positions near the stairwells and the elevators. It didn't look as if the hotel guests would have any choice.

O'Toole turned on the radio, and triumphant martial music flooded the room with drumbeats, blaring brass and piccolos. A stern announcer interrupted the merry melody.

"This is the military authority for the district of the capital city of La Paz. The present military action has been precipitated by a national security crisis. We ask the civilian population to stay calm and remain in their homes. The new president of the great Republic of Bolivia will address his people soon. Bolivians! Let us be inspired by the words of our national hymn. Propitious fate has crowned our hopes!"

O'Toole turned off the radio with a dour look just as the brass band returned to the air.

"Wonder who the new president is," he said to Barrabas.

There was another knock on the door, more urgent and authoritative than the hotel manager's. This time, Barrabas opened the door on a uniformed soldier of the Bolivian army. He wore a black armband with a red circle on his right arm and carried an old British EM-2 automatic rifle. On his head was a combat helmet. His face was stern and cold, too brittle for friendliness.

"I have been ordered to verify the passports of all guests in the hotel," he said quickly in an efficient monotone. His English had obviously been learned by rote.

"Oh, yes," Barrabas said slowly. "Come in. They're right over here."

The soldier stepped into the room, slightly disconcerted by the luxurious surroundings. He suddenly removed his helmet in an effort to be elegantly courteous before the rich tourists. Barrabas closed the door behind him. His passport was lying on the dresser.

"Liam, he's about your size, isn't he?" Barrabas asked, jerking his head toward the Bolivian soldier.

O'Toole nodded, a little puzzled. Barrabas picked up a porcelain lamp from the dresser and slammed the soldier across the back of the head. The lamp shattered into dozens of pieces. The soldier's eyes rolled into the back of his head, and he slumped to the floor.

Barrabas pulled the ancient EM-2 away from the soldier and looked it over. "Liam, welcome to the Bolivian army."

ALEX NANOS WAS HAVING A DREAM. He was running through the corridors of a resort hotel. Bombs, shrapnel and bullets exploded around him, their concussion waves buffeting him from all sides. Yet strangely, he was invulnerable. He passed through the middle of explosions that tore apart walls, but he didn't suffer the slightest wound.

Breathless, and with the stitch in his side scraping his gut raw, he wanted to stop, to rest and, above all, he wanted to eat. He looked over his shoulder. They were still there. A platoon of gleeful smiling women with long dark hair, draped in Uruguayan flags, chased him. Their big bare breasts swayed as they ran. And each one of them held a long deadly hatpin, tightly clenched between forefinger and thumb.

His eyes opened, and with a yell he sat up in bed.

The room was dark. A few lines of light glimmered faintly from behind the tightly closed curtain.

As if on cue, Billy Two entered from the adjoining room. Without looking at the Greek, he deposited himself in a chair and closed his eyes. Alex sighed, thankful that the dream was over. Most of it anyway. He was suddenly aware that the sounds of explosions and gunfire were still present, and growing louder.

"Hey, Billy!" What in hell's going on?"

The Indian ignored him. Not a muscle twitched.

Nanos threw back the covers, walked over and studied the Osage carefully.

"Billy Two? Billy Two!" He poked him in the chest. The Indian swayed slightly, but there was no other sign of life.

This time, Nanos grabbed him by the shoulders and shook. "Hey, Starfoot, wake the fuck up!"

Still no movement.

He walked quickly to the windows, flung back the heavy curtains and pushed out the shutters. He looked up a side street to the fighting in the Plaza Murillo just as a bullet nicked the window, shattering the glass and sending a shower of shards to the sidewalk two stories below.

"Holy shit!" He pulled the shutters in, bolted them and flung the drapes together for added protection. Then he ran back to the silent Osage.

"Billy Two!" He grabbed his buddy and shook harder. The Indian opened his eyes. He looked peeved. He raised his big hands, pressed them against Alex's chest and flicked.

The Greek tumbled, head over heels along the carpet.

"Hey!"

"Hawk Spirit has summoned me for consultation," Starfoot rumbled. "Do not disturb." He closed his eyes and went back to communing with his invisible friend.

There was a knock on the door.

Nanos picked himself up. "Weird," he muttered, curling his lip as he passed his buddy on the way to the door. He had barely turned the handle when Lee

Hatton and Nate Beck pushed urgently into the room.

"The place is crawling with them," Nate said to Lee.

"Yeah, let's see if we can see anything from here."

"What in hell's going on?" Nanos wailed plaintively.

"Alex, put on some clothes," Lee Hatton said. She pushed past him and went to the window.

Alex looked down. He was stark naked. Meekly he ran for his clothes, in a heap on the floor near the bed. "Will someone tell me what in hell's going on!" he begged, pulling his trousers up.

"Coup d'état," Nate replied succinctly, joining Lee at the window. They peered through the shutters.

"A military takeover," Hatton added. "We arrived the night before a revolution." Lee cast a quick glance in Billy Two's direction. "What's with him?"

"Him? Oh, him." Alex fumbled with the buttons on his shirt. "He's . . . you know. As usual."

There was a another knock on the door.

Nanos ignored it, and Lee walked to Billy Two and snapped her fingers once in his face. He opened his eyes, and a smile spread across his face like a sunbeam.

"Lee!" he said. "Good to see you."

Alex crossed the room and stood beside the team's medic, obviously at a loss. "How'd you do that?"

"It works every time. Snaps him right out of it."

The knocking on the door became persistent, and Alex crossed the room, muttering. "Of course, snap him out of it. Shaking doesn't work—"

A big husky soldier in combat fatigues filled the doorway. His helmet was pulled down low over his forehead and eyes. "I have orders to verify your passports," the man said with stern military authority. He stepped into the room and pushed the door shut behind him.

"Hey!" Nanos protested.

The soldier slipped his helmet off to reveal a head full of thick red Irish hair. "And a top o' the mornin' to you, too, folks!" O'Toole beamed, moving past Nanos to the center of the room. "Colonel's orders. Everyone needs a uniform and a gun. Then we're going to rob a bank. There's no cover like a little coup d'état."

Alex screwed up his face. "What the hell is going on?"

Nate walked over and put his hand gently on the Greek's back in a comradely gesture. "Alex, I know it's very early in the morning and you've barely got out of bed, so everything must seem terribly confusing to you."

"I haven't even eaten yet," Nanos added as an indication of his priorities.

"That's what I like about Alex," O'Toole boomed. "All he needs to be happy is a full belly and a woman in his bed."

"And I haven't had either for several days," Nanos protested.

"And the only time he's not complaining is when he's got a gun in his hands," Nate said with a wink to the others.

Alex shrugged off their taunts. "So? My needs are very basic."

"All right, cut the crap and let's get down to work," O'Toole told them, his voice rising to the pitch of a drill sergeant on the parade ground. "We need four uniforms of varying size. How are we going to get them? Do any of you have any bright ideas." The mercs looked at one another.

Lee stuck her neck out first. "You could use me."

The male mercs looked at her. Lee Hatton was a strikingly beautiful woman, with short, clipped dark hair, olive skin and brown eyes. She worked out frequently, and the muscled firmness of her strong slender body actually accentuated the female curves. But the khaki slacks and loose work shirt were hardly calculated to stun the male sex.

"I mean my body. As a lure. I don't mind. If you got it, use it, that's what I say. All's fair in love and war. Let them think it's love. For us it's war. Doesn't make any difference as long as we get their uniforms and their guns."

Alex coughed. "It's a great idea, Lee, but do you think these soldier boys are really going to go for the butch look?"

Lee nodded, half smiling. "You're right, Alex. It takes more than looks to catch a man." She walked into the bathroom and began grabbing towels off the racks. "It also takes low female cunning."

BARRABAS CHOSE A LOUD SPORT JACKET from his luggage and slipped it on. He checked himself in the mirror, smoothing his near-white hair and pulling the collar of his open shirt outside that of the jacket. All he needed now were white shoes to look like what he wanted to look like—the infamous loudmouthed tourist. Forget the white shoes. He didn't have any with him. He slipped into the hallway, looking quickly both ways. Two soldiers had taken up positions at the far end of the hallway, in the exit to the stairs. There were two more near the elevators. He moved silently into a nearby corridor that led through another wing of the grand old hotel and circled around to a second bank of elevators at the rear of the building.

"*¡Señor!*" a commanding voice ordered Barrabas to stop, and he turned around to see a tall officer of the Bolivian army marching toward him. This one wore a black armband, too. Obviously it identified the soldiers as belonging to one faction or another. It was impossible to say which ones were government and which were rebels. Nevertheless, this was definitely Barrabas's lucky day. Not only did the Bolivian carry a submachine gun and a holstered pistol, he was also Barrabas's height and build.

"Passport!" the man demanded with his hand out.

"Well, now," Barrabas drawled slowly with a big wide smile and lots of friendly teeth. "Seems I've left it in my room."

"It's forbidden to be in the corridors during the emergency. I will accompany you to your room."

"Well, that's great. Mighty friendly of you," Barrabas said, turning around and retracing his steps with the officer at his heels. "It's just down this way. My wife isn't feeling well. I promised to find someone who could help. You know how room service is on days like this, ha, ha."

The Bolivian soldier didn't laugh.

"What is the matter with your wife?"

"Damned if I know. Looks terrible. She can barely talk. Just kind of lies there in bed."

"I will examine her. If a doctor is necessary, one will be called."

"Well, thank you very much, Colonel. That's real kind of you. You are a colonel? I thought that's what all those ribbons on your shoulder meant. I used to be a colonel, too. American army."

They arrived at the door to Barrabas's room. He turned the key in the latch and pushed the door open.

"It's me, darling," Barrabas called.

The sheets were pulled up around a human figure sleeping in the bed. The Bolivian officer leaned over to have a look.

"But this is not—" was all the soldier managed to say.

The lamp Barrabas had used before had a double on the bedside table, and the merc lost no time in shattering it against the back of the officer's head. The man grunted and fell facedown on top of his bound and gagged army buddy in the bed.

"Sorry, pal," Barrabas said, bending over to strip the unconscious body. "It's just that you're wearing my size."

11

After the first one, the procedure became a routine assembly line.

By listening carefully, the mercs soon realized the soldiers made regular two-minute patrols of the hallways. Lee Hatton wrapped a big white towel around her head and threw the long end back as if her hair were wet. She stripped off her shirt and held another towel up to cover her chest. Then she peered around the open door into the hallway as one of the Bolivians came by.

She did a quick sizing up, gave finger signals to the others if it was go or no, one soldier or two or more, then she smiled and looked distressful.

"Oh, ah...*señor*..." By the time she was that far, the soldier turned toward her, his eyes revealing an eagerness to oblige the lady.

"*Ayudame, por favor.*" She backed into the room, and the Bolivian guard plunged headlong after her.

Nanos had concealed himself behind the door, and as the soldier charged into the room, the big Greek grabbed the soldier's helmet and threw him off-balance. One quick pull and the helmet was off. One quick flick of the wrist, and he smashed the helmet into the back of the soldier's head.

The Bolivian fell, unconscious. Hatton had closed the door after him, and O'Toole and Beck quickly scooped the soldier up and threw him on the bed beside the first one. Lee collected the guns, another British EM-2, and an old-fashioned Beretta M-51 handgun. From the well-oiled appearance of the growing collection, the weapons were standard Bolivian army issue.

"Hey, who's this one for?" Nanos was already wearing the Bolivian uniform they had taken from their first victim.

"Well, it sure isn't going to fit Billy Two," Lee said. "It's for Beck."

"Nothing's going to fit Billy Two." O'Toole said. "He takes up the space of an upright piano just standing there."

Lee Hatton looked up at the Osage's towering six feet six inches and massive barrel chest.

"That's what I'm worried about."

"It doesn't matter if I don't have a uniform." Starfoot declared solemnly. "I am invisible."

"Right, right," Nanos said as he nodded. "And I'm the new president of Bolivia. Let's get that guy's clothes off and get set up again."

Lee Hatton was the next one outfitted in the garb of Bolivia's finest. The proportions were a little off, particularly the jacket, but with the combat helmet pulled down low and the strap across her chin, she would pass.

"We could wait hours for someone big enough to go by who wears a uniform that'll fit Billy Two," Nate pointed out.

"That's right," said O'Toole. "Let's meet the colonel and see if we can pick up something on the way. All right, boys. Marching order. Ten-hut!"

BARRABAS MADE one last-minute adjustment to the collar of the trim tunic. The Bolivian officers wore spiffy uniforms. It made them look like they were made of the same stuff as all the medals they wore. Tin.

It was time to get started, and he decided to head for Nanos's room, or at least meet them halfway. At some point they'd all have to put their disguises to the test. It might as well be him, now.

"See ya, boys," Barrabas said as he flashed a quick nod to the still-unconscious Bolivian soldiers who lay bound and gagged on the floor.

He forced a stern expression onto his face, the kind that officers used to put the fear of God into the lesser ranks. It was just a matter of remembering back to those years of service in the U.S. Army, the years that had made him a powerful one-man show. A trained machine, coiled, wound up, primed to fight.

Professional soldier. Mercenary.

Nile Barrabas held the EM-2 in a ready position at his side. He knew the look he was carrying. It was a dare: Touch me, you're dead. The hallway was deserted except for the soldiers still in the stairwell at the far end. Walking swiftly and purposefully, he strode down the corridor in the opposite direction.

THE ONLY WAY TO DO IT was to look like they owned the place. O'Toole marched the Bolivian army's newest recruits briskly through the labyrinth of corridors in the old hotel.

Since Lee Hatton spoke Spanish, she marched in front, with O'Toole and Beck behind and Nanos following. Nate Beck's quick suggestion solved the problem of what to do with Billy Two. They made him a prisoner. The Osage warrior walked in the middle with his hands up.

The mercs had covered half the distance when they ran into a checkpoint. A battery of soldiers congregated near the main staircase. Eyes fixed straight ahead, the mercs tried as nonchalantly as possible to go by. The cold stares of the Bolivian soldiers followed them.

"*¡Alto!*" a young officer commanded them to halt. He moved away from the soldiers and stood in front of Lee, eyeing their prisoner. "There is a van on the street waiting to take the subversives for questioning," the Bolivian said, looking at Billy Two and motioning toward the stairs.

Hatton tensed her vocal cords in an effort to lower her voice an octave. She answered in perfect Spanish. "This is a special prisoner. A foreigner. I have special instructions regarding him."

The young officer's face clouded over with suspicion. "And what are these special instructions. From whom?" He regarded the other SOBs carefully as he spoke.

Tension tightened in the pit of Lee's stomach. Her mind raced for the right thing to say. The Bolivian slowly circled the mercs, looking at each of them. Billy Two stood quietly in the middle, a docile giant, with his face blank and his eyes far away.

O'Toole shifted uncomfortably. His eyes caught the Greek's in a careful sideways glance, and a warning passed between them. Neither man could understand the Spanish, but it was looking more and more as if they were going to have to fight their way out. The mercs tightened their grips on their automatic rifles and picked out their targets among the curious soldiers guarding the stairs.

The officer stopped in front of Hatton. "I think I'd better see your written orders," he said slowly, moving his hand to the holster at his waist and resting it on the butt of his pistol.

"Captain!" A second officer appeared from another corridor and addressed his subordinate sharply. The high black boots, trim pants and gold braid marked him as a high-ranking officer. His eyes were hidden behind the mirrored lens of his sunglasses.

The young captain turned abruptly, snapped his heels and saluted. "Sir!"

Lee had a sinking feeling that their sport was finished. Her back was turned to her fellow mercs, but she could sense their fingers inching toward the triggers of their automatic rifles. It was going to a free-for-all, and the only winners would be the bullets.

The senior officer returned the salute with a casual disregard. "Is there a problem with my prisoner, Captain?"

The stern, icy voice was familiar despite the fluent Spanish. Barrabas.

"No, Colonel. I was just about to verify the papers commanding the arrest of this man, since a vehicle waits below to transport prisoners to the stadium."

"This prisoner requires special handling. I'll take responsibility for him." Barrabas turned toward the soldiers guarding the stairs. "Have your men clear the way."

"Yes, sir. Immediately, sir."

The young Bolivian captain ordered his men to stand aside.

"Take the prisoner to the lobby," Barrabas ordered his mercs. He returned the captain's final salute and marched out beside them.

Outside, the battle continued.

The presidential palace had fallen to the rebels, and a portion of it burned. A sea of armed personnel vehicles, tanks and artillery spread halfway across the Plaza Murillo to sandbagged machine gun emplacements. The old Indian lady Barrabas had observed feeding pigeons lay facedown in a pool of spreading blood. Her pigeons and her seed were scattered and gone. Bullets rode the wind.

Most of the fire was aimed at the National Congress directly across the square. The Ministry of Revenue was also holding out. Soldiers loyal to the democratic government had barricaded the entrances to both buildings, turning them into fortresses of resistance. Soldiers fired from the windows of the upper stories while grenade launchers on the roof spat their deadly load. Smoke trails soared and crisscrossed high overhead, hovering above the plaza like a net.

The forces belonging to the junta rushed more and more soldiers into the square to set up artillery positions and unload missiles. Picked off by sudden clouds of shrapnel and snipers' bullets, their casualties were high. The cobblestone surface of their battleground was slick with blood.

Despite their withering fire, the troops loyal to the government were holed up like rats in a cave with no place to go. It was only a matter of time before the rebels were victorious. The air force was bombing parts of the suburbs, and flames and voluminous smoke drifted above the downtown streets. As the fighters that had destroyed the front of the presidential palace returned for a repeat performance against the National Congress, the SOBs left the hotel from the safety of a side entrance not far from the presidential palace.

"*¡Alto!*" Barrabas ordered.

The line of mercs stopped.

"Thanks, Colonel," Hatton told him. "You were in the right place at the right time."

"Now I know why we're unofficial," he said, looking at the uniforms on his men and Hatton. The dark green battle fatigues, high black boots and canvas straps were top quality. "Those monkey suits make all of you look honest."

Quickly he surveyed the plaza. They were well behind insurgent lines. The street was lined with military vehicles. Fiercely determined soldiers, urged on by their officers, streamed toward the front line in the Plaza Murillo.

"Left turn," Barrabas snapped at his soldiers. "And keep your heads up for trouble."

They were hardly noticeable in the general confusion in the streets around the Plaza Murillo. The

Banco Nacional was on the other side of the presidential palace, across the square from the hotel. So far, it seemed to have avoided the drama unfolding just beyond its steps. Its great front doors, now firmly closed, formed a wall of heavy bronze.

The armored personnel carriers that filled the street were French made VCIs—big, heavy and slow. Farther away, beyond the clouds of dark smoke billowing from the burning palace, Barrabas saw what he wanted—a Humber one-ton. Also known as "the Pig."

Originally built in a hurry by the British because of a shortage of armored transport vehicles during the Malaysian emergency, the Humber borrowed the chassis of a one-ton Rootes tactical vehicle. The Royal Ordnance factory had added another nine or ten tons of welded steel armor plating.

The result was a capacity-eight iron box with observation and firing ports on each side and in each of the double back doors. The big rubber tires were sheltered by steel fenders, and the windshields were small glass plates protected by wire covers. Its nickname came from its appearance. The cab of the Humber bore a definite resemblance to the face of a pig. The hood looked like a steel-clad snout, with narrow radiator slits for nostrils. Instead of a bumper, the front of the Humber was a sheet of steel plate, which began a few centimeters above the road and reached shoulder high to a man.

The newest recruits to the Bolivian army marched down the line of vehicles toward the rear of the presidential palace. Barrabas walked quickly into step next to Liam O'Toole. He spoke from the side of his mouth.

"Recognize it? Down there at the end of the street."

"Do I recognize it?" O'Toole spat suddenly. "Since I was knee high to a leprechaun. They've been a familiar sight in the streets of Belfast and Derry— at least until the Brits found out that high-velocity AP rounds can penetrate the hull."

"They've thrown in another couple of tons of armor modifications since then, Liam."

"And what vintage will they have here in Bolivia, sir?"

"Well, I guess we'll find out when they start shooting at us. Can you drive it?"

"Drive it! Where I come from they taught us in grade school, sir. I can drive it, or I can blow it up. Where to?"

"The bank."

"I don't think there's any parking on the Plaza Murillo right now, sir."

"That's okay, Liam. We'll take it inside with us." Barrabas ran ahead. "Double time!" he ordered in Spanish. Nanos, Beck and O'Toole took their cue from Lee Hatton and Billy Two. The line of mercs broke into a run.

The Humber idled near the curb. The two drivers paced outside the cab, nervously puffing on cigarettes and watching the fire fighters pour water on the presidential palace. The bulk of the Humber sheltered them against the thick smoke gusting from the burning wing. They both saw the tall officer leading his platoon of Bolivian soldiers through the acrid clouds.

"Hey, Manolo," one said to the other, pursing his lips and spitting a stream of cigarette smoke as if it were a cuss.

Manolo shrugged. "He's in such a hurry, he must be important."

"Ah. He can wait until we finish our cigarettes or find another truck to carry his prisoner. It's time for our break."

"I tell you an officer as important as this will have his own way." The one named Manolo laughed, flicking his cigarette to the ground and grinding it out.

Barrabas didn't wait to ask.

The mercs fanned out around the personnel carrier, bringing their autorifles to chest level, searching for anyone who might try to stop them.

Barrabas and O'Toole ran to the drivers and slapped them up against the hood of the Pig before they had a chance to ask why. Billy Two jumped in and stripped their guns away.

"Now I need them," he said, taking another EM-2 and two pistols, which he thrust into his belt. The two Bolivians were docile. They spread-eagled their arms and legs against the Humber, breathing quickly, their faces stiff with fear at the unexpected turn of events.

"Hustle, hustle!" Barrabas told the mercs, grabbing one of the prisoners by the arm and throwing him toward the rear of the armored carrier. "Get them in the back and tie them up."

Nanos and Beck grabbed the two soldiers and pushed them inside. Lee guarded the street, her eyes and nose stinging from the bitter smoke, until Billy Two arrived. Then she jumped in, and the mercs swung the heavy rear doors closed.

Barrabas climbed into the cab beside O'Toole. "Is it all here?" he asked.

The Irishman made a quick check of the double gears and the instrument panel. He nodded, trod on the clutch and slipped it into gear. The Pig grunted as it left the curb, chugging forward and slowly gaining speed.

"This might do sixty-five klicks an hour," he shouted over the noise of the engine. "How fast do you want me to be going when we hit those doors?"

"Liam, run it in there as fast as it'll go, and I hope she'll make it."

"She'll make it," O'Toole said confidently.

The flames ripping through the burning palace had retreated. The smoke gushing through the charred windows was ebbing as firemen directed their hoses against the building. The street behind the palace led to another one that emptied into the Plaza Murillo almost in front of the Banco Nacional. Explosions and automatic rifle fire roared around them as they approached the intersection.

O'Toole pulled the heavy APC past the fire trucks and turned right. The Plaza Murillo was still a battlefield, almost completely obscured by smoke from grenades and shelling. In the light blue sky far away, the fighters that had already done their damage to the presidential palace were small black darts against the pure white snow of the high Andes. They were growing bigger again very quickly. Like deadly needles, they zeroed in on the last stronghold of opposition—the National Congress. The mercs' target came up quickly on the left.

"I'm going to slam into it on an angle, sir," O'Toole said. "That way the point of impact against the doors will be in the center where they're weakest." Carefully he coordinated clutching and shifting to squeeze the last bit of speed out of the Pig.

The fighter jets came in low over downtown La Paz, faster than the speed of sound. Small orange sparks appeared under the hornet wings, and dark projectiles lanced toward the Plaza Murillo. Almost instantly, the facade of the National Congress blew into a flurry of smoke and debris. There was a momentary lull in the chatter of automatic rifle fire. Rebel soldiers jumped across their line in the Plaza and raced toward the embattled buildings.

O'Toole wound the steering wheel around and around with both hands until he forced the Humber to careen sharply to the left. The big heavy truck leaned onto two wheels. The huge rubber tires bit into the curb and rolled over the sidewalk. The front of the bank filled the field of vision from the narrow front windows of the Pig.

"Head down, Colonel, or you'll kiss the front doors through the windshield," O'Toole warned. Barrabas brought his knees up, put his arms against the dash and buried his head against them. The armored carrier struck with its left front corner.

The bronze gates buckled inward, crumpling like aluminum foil. There was a second impact as the Humber rammed the inner doors. Glass shattered and wood splintered. There was a spine-wrenching shriek from the transmission as O'Toole downshifted drastically and hit the brakes to halt the Pig's forward progress.

The Pig plowed across the marble floors, smashing aside chairs, desks, lamps and crushing everything in its path. It lurched to a halt, inches from a teller's wicket.

They were in.

Barrabas pushed himself up and yanked the handle on the side door. He swung out and jumped to the floor as the mercs poured from the back.

"Turn it around and block the entrance with it," he ordered O'Toole. Once again the Humber's engine roared as O'Toole repositioned the iron Pig.

The head office of the Banco Nacional was an enormous open area several stories high covered by a glass dome. On three sides long tellers' counters circled the room. Behind these were the executive offices, paneled with dark wood and filled with leather furniture. The mercs immediately fanned out, checking the offices for the presence of other personnel.

Lee Hatton appeared at the colonel's side.

"Are the prisoners secured?"

Lee nodded. "Billy Two's taking care of them with some rope."

The gray-haired man who had entered the bank from his limousine early that morning approached from the side, indignation bravely written across his face. Behind him, at the doorway to his office, two women were visible, cowering behind the door to his office.

"You have no right here!" he said to Barrabas in Spanish, waving his hands angrily. "We are a private business, and of no concern to the political struggle! Get out! Get out!"

A loud explosion outside drowned his words and shook the building savagely, shattering panes of glass in the dome overhead. Flakes of varnish filtered down from the walls, along with a rain of broken glass.

"We are here on behalf of the revolutionary government of Bolivia!" Barrabas replied, shouting over the noise of the continuing battle outside in the Plaza Murillo. "We have orders to seize the contents of a certain safety deposit box. Now!" He lifted his autorifle to make his threat perfectly clear.

The elderly banker blanched. His lips tightened with anger. It was obvious he had little choice. He turned stiffly. "The safety deposit boxes are on the lower level. Follow me."

Barrabas signaled for Hatton to follow. On the opposite side of the banking hall a wide staircase led down to a windowless marble foyer, faced on one side by a wall of iron bars. Beyond was a walk-in safe the size of a garage.

The banker pulled a ring of keys from his pocket, reluctantly unlocked the door in the wall of bars and slid it back.

"Now the safe," Barrabas told him.

"So Generalissimo Garcia Cheza has finally seized control," the man said, moving toward the safe. "The rumors we have been hearing for weeks have turned out to be true," the man said, moving toward the safe.

Nanos appeared at the bottom of the steps, and Barrabas walked to him quickly. They conversed in low voices, keeping their English inaudible to the Bolivian banker.

"Colonel, Liam's got the Pig parked just outside the entrance, but all hell's broken loose out there. The troops holed up in the government buildings are making a last-ditch attack, and there's hand-to-hand fighting going on in the Plaza. We took two secretaries and a caretaker prisoner. Billy Two and Beck are watching them."

"Okay, let's see what's cooking over here." The thick steel door of the safe was swinging open. The small room inside was lined with hundreds of metal drawers, each with two small locks.

"You have the keys?" Barrabas demanded of the banker.

"We have one key to each box. Naturally our clients maintain possession of the other key. If you do not have it, it will be impossible to open."

"What do you do if they don't pay their rent for the boxes?"

The banker twisted uncomfortably. "Of course, we must after a certain length of time, and having made every effort to inform them, er...ah...remove the locks. But this is illegal. The client must sign a card and bring his own key. Otherwise, it is robbery!"

"The safety deposit box in question contains valuable information concerning the vital interests of Bolivia. It is a national emergency. How do you remove the locks? If necessary, we will use explosives."

The banker hesitated, weighing his choices. "We drill them out," he said finally.

"Who does it?"

"Well, er... the caretaker usua—"

Barrabas turned to Hatton. "Get him," he ordered. "How long does it take?"

"Perhaps half an hour. Perhaps twenty minutes."

"He has ten. After that, we blow it open."

12

A convoy of a FV-1 Spartans slowed to a halt outside the presidential palace, and a procession of Bolivian military brass emerged from the armored jeeps. Generalissimo Garcia Cheza looked briefly over his shoulder at the tumult on the Plaza Mayo. Aides rushed to his side and ushered the new president of the Bolivian Republic away from danger.

"Generalissimo, the part of the palace containing your office has not been damaged," Colonel Alvara de Candia, Cheza's aide-de-camp, told him as he entered the executive mansion. "And the fire in the other wing is almost out."

"Excellent," Cheza replied. "And the telephones?"

"Service has been restored, sir. The elite troops trained by Señor Barbier have seized the telephone exchanges, the radio and television stations and the electrical compounds throughout the major cities. Our own troops have almost eliminated resistance at the National Congress and the university. Only the Indian workers at the tin mines are holding out.''

''Send reinforcements. I want them suppressed at once.''

''*Sí*, Generalissimo.'' The military aide whispered the orders to an officer who in turn passed the order to another. The whisper was passed down a line of ranking officers until one ran off to execute the order. Cheza strode briskly through the shattered corridors of the palace. Furniture was overturned, and doors opened onto ransacked offices, bearing witness to the hasty departure of the previous tenants. It reeked of smoke, and water from the firemen's hoses was several inches deep, running over the carpets and lapping at the general's polished black boots.

Some of his aides ran ahead of him to open the double doors that led into the presidential office. There, at least, the damage had been cleared away. Cheza surveyed the room briefly, mildly impressed by its elegance. He had come a long way since his years as a mediocre student at Bolivia's finest military college. But his wealthy family, which owned cocoa plantations in the Andean lowlands, had prepared him for such eventualities.

He pulled the chair out from the president's desk and sank into it with a satisfied air. It was comfortable. He liked it. The sounds of battle outside were fading.

"My friends!" Cheza smiled, holding up his hands in exclamation as the other officers gathered in the room. "The coup d'état is complete! We are now the masters of our country. *¡Viva la República Boliviana!*"

"*¡Viva la República Boliviana!*" the officers, led by Alvara de Candia, shouted in unison.

A young lieutenant entered the room. "Generalissimo!" he said urgently. "Commander Schicklgruber of the Fiancés of Death wishes an immediate audience, sir!" Cheza smiled to the others in the room, and they seemed to share his amusement, although as Cheza well knew, they were ignorant of its source.

This man Schicklgruber was a recent import from Europe, with a past that included questionable criminal activity. He was a mousy, sniveling young man, dreaming of long-lost Nazi glory. Like Barbier and von Rausch, whom he served, this Schicklgruber saw the Bolivian coup as the beginning of a new Nazi empire.

The elite squad called the Fiancés of Death was a concession to the German expatriates who had helped the generals plan and execute the coup d'état. With the success of the putsch, their assistance was no longer required. Now the generals had other interests—the main one being the monopoly on profits from the cocaine trade.

As for Generalissimo Garcia Cheza, President of the Republic of Bolivia, he had his own goals to pursue.

"Show him in," Cheza ordered.

Almost immediately a short, slight man with the shadow of a Hitler moustache on his top lip strutted into the presidential office.

"*Heil*, Generalissimo Cheza!" he shouted, flapping his arm straight up in the air and snapping his heels together.

"Commander Schicklgruber, I congratulate you on the victories of your brave soldiers this morning."

"They have struck like lightning!" Schicklgruber announced in a monotone. "They have crushed all opposition mercilessly!"

The general looked at his nails. "There was an urgent matter you wished to discuss?" he asked quietly.

Schicklgruber looked at the general and at the other Bolivian military officers around the room, for a moment uncertain if this was the right time or place.

"Come, come, Commander," Cheza coaxed, noticing the German's hesitation.

From the breast pocket of his black military shirt, Schicklgruber pulled out a sheet of paper and unfolded it. He handed it to Bolivia's new president and remained stiffly at attention.

"One hundred and eighty-five names of subversives, Generalissimo, prepared for us by the effective agents of DINA, the Chilean secret police under the command of eminent Herr von Rausch! My troops are prepared to begin their elimination!"

Cheza scanned the long list of names. There were opposition politicians, university professors, journalists, students, writers, artists, poets, trade unionists, judges, even social workers—all the people to be expected on such a list.

"But him, he is a professor of paleontology at the university!" the general said, pointing to one name.

"A liberal, Excellency Generalissimo Cheza. Very dangerous." Schicklgruber swallowed, his eyes darting nervously at the faces of the Bolivian officers.

"But he is my cousin," the general objected. "And that one is my uncle. And here, she is my wife's aunt. No, no, it is impossible. These are all my relatives," he said, waving his hand at the list.

It was true. Most of the wealthy and the educated of Bolivia were related through blood or marriage.

A brief titter of barely suppressed laughter rippled through the room. Schicklgruber reddened from both anger and embarrassment.

"But these people will endanger the revolution, Generalissimo. Why, Herr Barbier has assured our troops that blood would flow. You yourself saw a demonstration of the method of execution. It requires only your order for the mobile gas chamber to be brought to La P—''

''Enough!'' Cheza shouted, obviously annoyed by Schicklgruber's pleading. ''I have said it is impossible. We will ensure the survival of my regime through other, equally effective methods of suppression. Tell that to your master, Señor Barbier. Now leave me!''

He stood and waved his arms, not only at the astonished Schicklgruber, but at everyone. The commander of the Fiancés of Death, and the Bolivian officers, appeared momentarily uncertain of their next move.

''Leave me, all of you! I have presidential duties to attend to!'' As Cheza's voice rose, they hastily retreated. Colonel Alvara de Candia waited at the door after the others had gone. ''Generalissimo?''

''Out!'' Cheza roared.

Alvara de Candia jumped. He closed the door promptly behind him. When Cheza was finally alone, he took a small vial from his pocket and poured two long lines of white powder on the polished desk. He lowered his face and inhaled sharply through one nostril at a time until both lines had disappeared. The row of shiny medals dangling on ribbons from his chest clanged against the edge of the desk. He sat up and sniffled a moment. Then he felt better. Much better.

He took a deep breath and examined his surroundings as the drug took effect. As the new president of his country, he felt wonderful. He looked at his shiny medals. He wanted more. It was simple enough now for him to award himself the coveted Medal of Honor. Or to create a new order even. The Order of Meritorious Courage. He liked the sound of it. A ruby set in a platinum medal would look nice.

He was looking forward to his presidential duties. He picked up the telephone. There was a dial tone. Good. It was working. Colonel Alvara de Candia came on the line.

"I wish to speak to the President of the Banco Nacional. Yes, right away. It concerns the country's reserves of gold and foreign currency."

As he spoke, he fished in his pocket for a small slip of paper with a twelve-digit number written on it. "Yes. Immediately," Cheza instructed his aide. "I have here the number of a Swiss bank account...."

BARRABAS FELT THE TENSION building steadily among the SOBs as the sounds of battle outside the bank diminished. The president of the bank fidgeted nervously, still angry about the violation of his code of business behavior.

Only the caretaker remained cool. Slowly and methodically, the old man assembled a circular diamond-edged bit in the electric drill and placed it over the lock. The vault filled with the acrid odor of burning metal as the high-speed drill ground through the resistant alloy.

Barrabas checked his watch. Eight minutes. The president noticed and looked worried. The caretaker lifted the drill away and examined the safety deposit box. Wordlessly he took a rubber mallet and a steel chisel from his toolbox.

There were footsteps on the stairs, and Lee Hatton burst into the vault. She waved Barrabas aside and spoke quietly.

"Colonel, the radio just announced the fall of the government, and guess who's already on the phone? Someone from the office of the new president of the Republic wants to talk to the president of the bank."

"Take him upstairs, but monitor the conversation carefully. He still thinks we're from the government, and I'd like to keep it that way. Don't do anything that might put him on guard. But at the same time, don't let him say anything that might jeopardize us." Barrabas turned to Beck. "Nate, can you set the timer on the vault lock?"

"Sure," the computer wizard nodded. "It's primitive technology."

"Lee, bring the secretaries and the two soldiers from the Humber down here. We'll lock them up for a couple of hours."

Lee walked the bank president up the wide stairs to the main floor, then followed him into his office. The two women, who sat nervously in chairs, were clearly relieved at the sight of their employer. Alex Nanos stood over them, fidgeting with his gun. He turned as Lee and the bank president entered. He looked as white as a ghost.

"You okay?" Lee whispered.

Nanos shook his head. "I feel like my head's going to explode, and I'm short of breath. I dunno why. I never feel this way. Is it the thin air, Doc?"

Lee nodded. "Yeah. Hang in there, Alex. It's slowing us all down. You'll be okay?"

The Greek winked and cast her a carefree grin. "If I can survive the lady with the hat pin, what's a bit of oxygen deprivation?"

The elderly president of the Banco Nacional went to his desk and lifted the phone. Lee stood beside him, listening carefully. He looked at her, his dark eyes filled with resentment, and he shook with barely controlled fury at the violent intrusion into his bank. *"Sí,"* he said grimly into the receiver.

In his office in the presidential palace, Colonel Alvara de Candia spoke to the president of the Banco Nacional, quickly explaining the gold and currency transfers the new Bolivian leader wanted made.

"But that's impossible!" the banker exclaimed. "It will ruin the country. The economy will collapse!"

"My orders are explicit," Alvara de Candia said adamantly. "You will do as instructed. I will send a party of soldiers to remove the gold and currency immediately. Make sure that it is ready for them when they arrive.''

The bank president trembled with anger at his country's new masters. ''Don't bother sending over any more soldiers,'' he said coldly. Then he added, too quickly for Hatton to stop him, ''The ones who are here now can take it with them when they leave.''

He slammed the receiver down and looked up at Hatton, his eyes icy with hatred. ''Your officers will destroy this country,'' he said. His anger was gone, replaced by sadness and resignation.

In the presidential palace, Alvara de Candia looked at the telephone receiver. He was not personally aware that the general had already sent soldiers to the bank. What for? he wondered.

He left his desk and went to the shattered window. The battle on the Plaza Murillo had ended. The square was littered with corpses, and fire was rapidly reducing the National Congress to a charred ruin. Autofire still echoed through the streets of La Paz as the army put down the last of the resistance. He leaned out and looked down the heavily damaged facade of the palace, which afforded him a narrow view of the front of the Banco Nacional.

There was an armored personnel carrier just outside the front doors. Something gnawed at him. A feeling that all was not quite right.

Colonel Alvara de Candia moved slowly back to his desk, deep in thought. He stood to gain a great deal from the successful execution of the Bolivian coup d'état. He stood to gain even more if his suspicions proved correct and the Banco Nacional was being robbed. The general would be very pleased with him when he learned that he had saved Bolivia's gold and foreign currency reserves from the greedy depredations of lowlife vermin. As for the perpetrators of the theft, the orders of the junta were explicit. Looters were to be summarily executed.

He made his decision and reached for the telephone.

"Hello, Captain Carbone? Put together a party of ten soldiers, heavily armed. Right away. I will command them personally. In front of the presidential palace. Yes, immediately."

THE CARETAKER PLACED THE CHISEL squarely on top of the lock. He began hitting the handle with sharp, steady blows from the mallet.

Lee Hatton appeared at the door of the vault with the bank president and the two frightened secretaries in tow. She ushered them quickly to the back of the vault and motioned Barrabas to step aside.

"I think we're in a heap of trouble, Colonel," Hatton told him, quietly recounting the telephone conversation.

"Bring the other two prisoners down here. Tell the others to get into the Humber and be ready to pull out."

"Colonel!" Nate Beck entered the vault. "The timer's set. Once we close the door the locks won't be released for two hours."

The caretaker swung the rubber mallet again and the small round lock suddenly popped from its metal casing into the drawer.

"For the second lock there is the key," the Bolivian said, methodically putting away his tools.

"The key." Barrabas put his hand out to the president of the Banco Nacional. The elderly banker handed it to him.

Billy Two appeared at the door of the vault. Over each mammoth shoulder he carried one of the Humber's original drivers, bound securely with rope and gagged. One had been stripped to his underwear. The six-foot-six Osage now wore a Bolivian army uniform at least four sizes too small. The sleeves of the jacket ended just below his elbow, and the pant legs halfway down his calves. The seams of the fabric were ready to split.

"Now I have a uniform, too," he announced the obvious.

"Good, Billy. Put them in the corner and join the others in the Humber," Barrabas told him.

The Indian walked to the back of the vault, glancing balefully at the astonished bank employees. He shucked the two soldiers off his shoulders, letting them fall heavily to the floor.

Barrabas inserted the banker's key in the second lock on the safety deposit box. It turned smoothly, and the little metal door opened easily. Nate lifted a heavy metal box the size of a briefcase from the drawer.

"Okay, get it out of here," Barrabas ordered. He turned at the door of the vault to face the banker and the other prisoners. "Two hours," he told them. "Then the door will open and you'll be free."

"You are not from the revolutionary government after all, are you?" The banker's question was somewhere between suspicion and relief. "Who are you?"

"I can't tell you that. All I can say is that I wish no harm to your country. But on that score you have to trust me."

Barrabas left the vault and pushed the huge door shut behind him. Beck placed the safety deposit box on a table outside. He lifted the hinged lid and threw it back. On top was a neat stack of typewritten material, with marginal notes in Walker Jessup's handwriting. Barrabas lifted them out and flipped quickly through them. There were lists of names, briefing papers, details of the Bolivian economy and other information that was useless to him. Then he came to what he was looking for.

He recognized the mug shots stapled to the documents even before he read what Jessup had written beneath them.

The first was Karl Barbier, the infamous "Butcher of Brussels," an escaped war criminal who had disappeared into South America in the late 1940s. He was on the Israeli secret service's hit list and had been sentenced to death in absentia by the war crimes trials in Europe. There was a bounty of a million dollars on his head, offered by various European governments and war victim organizations.

Next was Adolf von Rausch. Once he had been the SS governor of all the Baltic states under German occupation during the war. He had directed the mass executions of opponents of the Nazi regime. Somehow von Rausch had gotten away with his crimes. He worked for DINA, the Chilean secret police, one of the most vicious agencies of its kind in the world—in large part due to Rausch's expertise.

None of this was new information. But the map showing the Institute of Linguistic Semantics was. And Jessup's hastily scrawled notes dated several days before the attacks on the SOBs had begun were chilling.

"It's all here," Barrabas said. "Everything we need. The answer to our problems over the last few days is about an hour's drive outside the city."

"Will we take the Pig?"

"Sure. We may run into roadblocks on the way. If we can't bluff our way out of La Paz, at least we can ram our way through." Barrabas folded the briefing papers in half and shoved them inside his shirt. "There's a telex machine upstairs, isn't there?"

Beck nodded. "A whole row of them. If they're working. The telephones are up so they should be."

"Let's get going. I want to get a message to Bishop and Hayes in Arequipa before we leave here."

"What's in this?" Beck asked, pulling a cardboard document case from the safety deposit box.

"Open it."

Beck pulled the elastic straps away and unwound the string that kept the lid down. He turned the top back and looked inside. A low whistle escaped from between his teeth.

Sixteen crisp, neat wads of American thousand-dollar bills stared up at them. Barrabas picked one up and flicked the edges of a hundred notes like a deck of cards.

"How much?" Beck asked.

"One point six million," Barrabas answered without counting. It was amazing how such a small amount of paper could be so valuable. The Fixer's blood money. Poor Walker Jessup. This time, the blood was his own.

LIAM O'TOOLE KEPT HIS EYES on the street, his back to the door frame, and held the EM-2 across his chest. Sporadic gunfire sounded from distant directions throughout the city like firecrackers being set off in back alleys.

A ghostly tranquillity spread eerily across La Paz as columns of smoke spiraled silently upward among the high rises of the city's skyline. The morning resumed, apparently normal, as if the coup d'état were just a hiccup in the daily routine.

O'Toole fought a sense of growing urgency, a feeling in his gut that the sooner they were out of there the better.

"Liam!" Lee Hatton ran to O'Toole, stopping a moment to catch her breath before she spoke.

"You feel it, too?" O'Toole asked.

Lee nodded. "Fatigue. It's from the lack of oxygen in the air. We're lucky if that's all we suffer. It normally takes two or three days to go from sea level to twelve thousand feet. I'm worried about Alex. He doesn't look too good. He's suffering from altitude anoxia. So far he's only feeling headache and some nausea. If it gets worse, we could see a pretty sick guy."

"How sick?"

"Hallucinations."

Billy Two, who resembled an oversize scarecrow in the tiny Bolivian army uniform, was crossing the banking floor toward the armored carrier with Alex Nanos. The Greek was still pale and dragging his feet.

"Is the colonel almost done down there?" the Greek asked slowly.

"Yeah," Hatton confirmed. She turned back to O'Toole. "He wants the Pig started up and ready to pull out."

"Welcome words to my ears," Alex said with visible relief as O'Toole moved toward the cab of the armored carrier. He had barely turned when four army jeeps screamed to a stop on the street outside the bank. A dozen Bolivian soldiers armed with submachine guns leaped out and fanned around the mercs.

"*¡Alto!*" an officer shouted, racing toward the doors of the Banco Nacional. "Freeze! Put your hands up!"

Trapped by the surprise attack, the mercs raised their hands slowly but kept their grip on the EM-2s. The Bolivian soldiers stood only a few feet from them as the officer stepped closer for an inspection. His eyes were immediately drawn to Billy Two. "You are a big stupid-looking oaf," Colonel Alvara de Candia said to the Osage, smiling maliciously. "You can tell Andean peasant stock. They are strong, but basically a lesser breed lacking intelligence."

"We are under orders—" Lee began, faultlessly lowering her voice an octave.

"No orders have been issued regarding the Banco Nacional!" Alvara de Candia interrupted with a shout. "Take their weapons!"

The Bolivian officer stood back a step while his soldiers jammed the barrels of their submachine guns against the mercs' bodies. They ripped the EM-2's from their hands and stripped the pistols from their holsters. The four mercs were forcibly spun around and pushed face first against the Humber.

"Sergeant!" Alvara de Candia shouted to one of his men. "Form a firing squad!"

13

A shaft of sunlight, thin as a pencil, beamed through a pin-sized hole in the corrugated tin covering the tiny window. Otherwise the cell was dark.

Walker Jessup pushed himself up from the hard cement floor and tried to press his eye to the little hole. Once again he saw nothing but a stockpile of oil drums and behind them the snow-covered peak of an Andean mountain.

He tried to steady himself as the familiar sense of vertigo returned and the room began an unsteady circular swim around his head. The spells were less frequent now, and not as severe as they had been when he had returned to consciousness two days ago. But they still had a punch. Thousands of volts of electric pain shot up his arm to his shoulder when he grabbed the windowsill. They had shoved needles into his arm like spigots into a cask of beer. He slumped to the floor to wait for the dizziness to pass.

He had completely lost track of time. He might possibly have been a prisoner for a few days, but it could just as easily be a month or more. He had no idea how long they had kept him drugged, or what they had used, but the aftereffects had all the telltale indications of sodium pentothal. Truth serum. They had pumped him full of it and had probably drained out everything he knew. About what? It was a question he had asked himself a hundred times already. Between the time he had been whisked away from his hotel to the moment he had awakened, weak and nauseous and barely able to think, he recalled nothing.

His clothes, torn and filthy, hung on his once massive frame like a tent. What the hell, he told himself, getting to his feet once again. Might as well make the most of the fringe benefits. Loosing weight was an age-old promise to himself that he never kept. He breathed sharply to clear his head and leaned over, making a gargantuan effort to touch his toes. He came within five inches. Not bad, he congratulated himself. Before he had been brought here, he couldn't even see them when he looked down.

He bent over, stretching toward his toes five more times before standing upright and attempting a sustained burst of running on the spot. Knees up, knees up, he huffed and puffed as the sweat broke out on his forehead and dripped down his nose. When he finished, his chest was heaving.

He waited, counting the seconds with his mental clock. At sixty he threw himself to the floor and tried push-ups, fighting against the pain that rippled through the needle-sore muscle of his right arm. For the first time in the three days since he had began his regimen, he got all the way up before collapsing into an exhausted heap. One, he thought. Give yourself one, just for encouragement.

He flipped onto his back, squeezed all his determination into his gut and with enormous effort managed five sit-ups. Yesterday he had only been able to do three. Things were looking up. It was his last wish. Since he was probably going to die, maybe he would at least die in good physical condition. It all depended on how long his captors decided to let him live.

A little voice inside his head said, "Don't kid yourself, Walker." He was doing it because he knew the only way to survive prison isolation was to give yourself a goal—to remember everybody you've known in your entire life, to recall a book word for word from memory, to compose your autobiography—and pour every ounce of willpower into that one obsession. He was doing it because he wanted to live.

There was noise and laughter outside the door of the little cell, and a key rattled in the tin-covered door. He heard one of his jailers shouting, and he sat up.

The door opened, and an olive-skinned Hispanic stepped inside the cell. He pointed the automatic rifle he carried at Walker Jessup. He was still laughing from the memory of a recent joke, and his white teeth flashed in the darkness.

"You come now," he said in English. Outside the cell, somewhere in the prison, the guard's buddy shouted in Spanish.

"León, you need help?"

"Naaa," the guard yelled back. "The fat man is no problem." He turned, standing by the open door, and laughed at Jessup once again. "They are ready for you. Say goodbye to your last home."

Jessup looked at him uncertainly.

"Come on. Get up," the guard commanded. He motioned for the Fixer to step out of the cell.

Jessup thought about it for a few seconds and decided now was as good a time as any. He pushed himself slowly up from the floor and, when his legs were under him, he pitched forward, using his head as a battering ram.

"Ooommmph!"

He connected heavily with the guard's solar plexus, knocking the Bolivian against the wall on the other side of the corridor and driving the air from his diaphragm. Better still, he was on top, and he had the gun.

The guard gasped for breath and struggled feebly. Jessup had lost weight, but he was still a load. He balled his fist, gritted his teeth and clobbered the guard's head, aiming his knuckles for the soft spot at the temples. The guard's eyes glazed over, but not fast enough. Jessup lifted the rifle and bashed it into the man's face. His eyes rolled one full turn in their sockets, then closed for the season.

The Fixer crouched over the body and listened. No sound. He looked down the corridor. Its walls were blank and opened into a second one running perpendicular some ten meters away. The one light bulb was dark behind its screen covering.

He quickly felt through the man's pockets, removing a small knife and an extra magazine. In a breast pocket he found a real treasure. A cigar and a package of matches. Cautiously, quietly, he stood, pocketing his finds. With his right hand clasped firmly around the guard's old British EM-2, he tiptoed quickly to the end of the corridor and peered around the corner. The second man was sitting on a stool facing the other way, near the door that led outside. The distance between them was barely six feet.

How quietly can I tiptoe? Jessup asked himself. The answer came out of somewhere. Either real quiet, or never again. He lifted his heels and ventured on his toes into the corridor, holding the rifle by its stock and swinging it over his head. He felt like an elephant on a tightrope.

Jessup didn't waste time. What he lacked in delicacy he made up for in speed. The guard heard him. He turned.

The guard's jawbone drove past his ears as he somersaulted off the stool and into the wall. He kicked as he tumbled, screaming and grabbing his jaw. To fall was death. Jessup raised the rifle and swung again. It made a dull, sickening thud as it bashed the soldier's head open like a grape. For a moment the Fixer recoiled. Then he heard the big voice from the sky say, Jessup, you win. Suddenly he felt great. He headed for the door.

The sight that met his eyes outside almost knocked him out. He stepped out onto the windswept plateau that appeared to float in blueness between the craggy snow-covered peaks of the high Andes. The great rocky giants stood just beyond the rim of land, appearing to gaze solemnly down at the buildings of the Institute for Linguistic Semantics like stone judges.

The wind was strong and chilly and blew yellow dust into the air as it hissed and whistled through eaves and around corners. The wide grassy quadrant and the lanes between the one-story buildings were deserted. Windows, like blank unlidded eyes, stared at him from everywhere. Panic's bony hand clutched Jessup's heart. He forced himself to think.

He remembered the barrels. If his sense of direction was accurate, the storage compound was to his left. It offered, if nothing else, a hiding place. Standing out on the exposed plateau, he half expected the hand of some god he had offended to reach down from heaven and point him out.

The Fixer edged quickly to the left and backed down the side of the building. The edge of the plateau wasn't far away, and it was clearly a sharp drop, perhaps hundreds of meters. He knew there was a narrow road winding through the mountains to La Paz, but it wasn't in his vicinity. He made a run across open space to the first row of oil drums and darted behind them.

It was a storage area for some kind of chemicals. Hundreds of multicolored steel barrels were piled in a large area adjacent to the loading entrances of a long building. Some of the stacks were almost twenty feet high, in long rows of twenty or thirty. They were also clearly marked. Acetone and ether.

The Fixer recognized a cocaine-processing plant when he saw one. He also knew highly volatile, highly flammable liquids. He looked up at the mountains with a sigh, and they seemed to look back in approval.

His chances of getting off this mountain plateau alive were slim, but acetone and ether offered a great opportunity for some explosive action and further fireworks. Lady Luck had, by chance, provided him with everything he needed to improvise a primitive time fuse. If he was fortunate, he could create a diversion. If he wasn't, well, what the hell, the Texan thought. If you can't get fat, go out with a bang.

BARRABAS HEARD THE COMMOTION at the door of the Banco Nacional as he and Nate crossed the banking hall. For a moment he thought he had choices—the first, to bluff it through as a Bolivian colonel. But it unfolded too fast, with the mercs pushed against a wall and eight soldiers in a row with their rifles up.

It would have to be the second choice. He hit the trigger of the EM-2 as he was running. A stream of spent casings popped from the side as the bullet explosions reverberated through the stock. He slid across the marble floor, tightening his grip against the recoil and forcing the barrel into line. The magazine emptied, zigzagging in bloody holes across the chests of the surprised firing squad. The line tumbled down like bowling pins.

Just as Barrabas's mag emptied, the death chatter from Nate Beck's autorifle began its refrain. He ran ahead of the colonel, swinging wide to the side as Bolivian soldiers poured into the entrance. Beck squeezed the trigger and moved the gun back and forth, spraying a hot mag across the doorway. The soldiers danced weirdly, quickly, and dropped.

Outside, the mercs rearmed themselves as Colonel Alvara de Candia retreated with his few remaining soldiers behind the cover of a jeep. Bullets spat and whined around them, twanging like wire between the guns on both sides.

"Behind the Humber!" O"Toole shouted, pushing Hatton ahead of him. Billy Two grabbed Nanos around the chest with a long, thick arm and hauled him over.

"What in hell are you doing?" Nanos demanded as he struggled against the Osage's viselike grip. Billy Two put him down and ignored him.

"I am going to take care of this man who called me an oaf," he announced, standing. He ran quickly to the front of the Pig and looked carefully around the bumper. Colonel Alvara de Candia and his men had run to cover behind the jeeps parked on the road. One of them was reaching through a door to grab the radio transmitter from the instrument panel as Billy Two flicked his rifle on semiauto, raised the barrel and sighted. He squeezed once quickly. A single bullet struck the man's hand and chunked into the control panel. The man yelped, and the hand disappeared. Now there was no noise or movement.

"Billy Two!" The Osage looked behind him. O'Toole was waving him to come back. He shook his head.

The Plaza Murillo was almost deserted. Except for columns of smoke from burning buildings and vehicles, and abrupt skirmishes of rifle fire from the direction of the National Congress, all was calm and quiet. But soon the shooting at the Banco Nacional would attract attention. There were four jeeps parked in front of the bank, and the Bolivians were hidden behind the first one.

Billy Two crouched. I am invisible in battle, he told himself. It was a promise that Hawk Spirit had made to him. He moved silently across the sidewalk, prowling like a cat in the shadows.

"What's he doing?" Barrabas demanded of O'Toole. He was pressed against the wall just inside the front doors of the Banco Nacional, watching for movement from behind the row of empty jeeps. Sprawled in front, the bullet-riddled corpses were twisted into bizarre death postures. It was almost quiet enough to hear the sidewalk soaking up the blood.

O'Toole stood behind the armored carrier with the other mercs. He looked at Barrabas with unconcealed exasperation. "He won't take orders, Colonel, not when he gets all heated up in the midst of battle. That crazy Indian'll just get himself killed."

"If he's making his own decision, then it's his problem. Right now I just want to flush out the rest of those soldiers behind the jeeps."

"Any thought about how we're getting out of here after that?"

"It's all taken care of. Bishop and Hayes are picking us up in a helicopter in two hours."

"Well, it promises to be an exciting wait. And where are we meeting them?"

"See that mountain up there?" Barrabas motioned toward the hulking snow-covered massif of Illimani. "On the other side of that, about an hour out of La Paz."

"We take the limousine?" O'Toole jerked his thumb at the squat ugly Pig.

"Yup. And one of those jeeps. The one with the machine gun mounted in back. But I have a feeling there are a few guys out there who might object. Any suggestions?"

"Use the Pig."

Barrabas nodded. "Let's do it."

Billy Two crouched between the fenders of two of the jeeps. He peered around the bumper and saw the three Bolivian soldiers who had survived the onslaught. One of them was binding up the hand of the officer who had called him an oaf.

As silently as smoke, the Osage moved into the street and came up behind them. He spread his arms wide, and his shadow fell over the side of the jeep. Alavara de Candia turned. Billy Two stood over him like the specter of darkness moving across the face of the sun. The Indian's big hands closed around the heads of the two Bolivians soldiers.

He clapped, bashing their heads ferociously together with Alavara de Candia's head in the middle. There was a spine-chilling thud of bone smashing against bone. Alavara de Candia's eyes closed, and he pitched forward, a plume of blood gushing from his nose.

Suddenly the Humber armored carrier rolled forward from the doors of the bank and smashed across the sidewalk into the jeeps at the curb. The gun ports on the sides bristled with automatic rifles. The Humber careened left as the steel plate at the front swept the vehicles into the street, tipping one onto its side.

O'Toole braked abruptly and pulled up beside Billy Two. Barrabas and Nate Beck jumped down from the other side and ran around the front of the carrier.

"Thanks for taking care of them, Billy!" O'Toole shouted over the noise from the engine. "You can let them go now."

Billy looked down. He still had his big hands clasped around the heads of the Bolivian soldiers. He dropped them. They flopped limply to the street. O'Toole put the Pig in gear and drove into the streets of La Paz.

Barrabas flew past, slapping the Indian on the arm and climbing into the driver's seat of the jeep.

"Let's go, Billy."

"Where to?" Billy asked, climbing into the seat beside Nate Beck. Their leader started up the jeep and pulled into the street.

"To the other side of the mountain. And for the next two hours, the machine gun mounted on the tripod behind us is all yours."

The Indian snorted. "Machine gun is for pale-faces. I have these." He held up his immense hands and flexed them into fists. "Besides," he mumbled. "I am invisible."

14

The cocaine generals raised their glasses to the toast proposed by Karl Barbier.

"To your great victory today, generals. And to the foundation of the new Axis empire."

"Bravo! Bravo!" several of them shouted as the gathering of the Bolivian brass threw back the shot glasses of schnapps.

"Gentlemen, now that Generalissimo Cheza sits in the presidential palace on the Plaza Murillo, we have only a few loose ends to clean up. I invite you to another demonstration of our friend Rausch's vehicle—public transit as it were, except there's no transfer and no return ticket."

There were quietly appreciative laughs.

"The merchandise today," Barbier continued, "is...well, it's not important really. An informant of sorts, although he was mildly unwilling to inform initially, if you know what I mean."

Again the generals chuckled knowingly.

"In any event, this merchandise promises to be more entertaining because, instead of two pieces of normal size, this one is extra large.'' Barbier winked, and the generals snickered.

The former Gestapo chief glanced quickly at his watch. He had sent the soldier a while ago. Jessup should be in front of the building by now.

''Gentlemen, please,'' he said, gesturing with open arms toward the door. The generals began to file past. ''Perhaps we can wager, gentlemen. On how long it will take...''

The van waited, the engine idling. Several soldiers stood at attention in front of it. The camp was quiet. The Fiancés of Death had gone to La Paz to assist in the seizure of the National Congress. The barracks housed only a skeleton crew. Since it was diplomatically unwise for von Rausch to be in Bolivia on the day of the coup, he had returned to Santiago.

Barbier glanced toward the prison building at the far end of the camp. A chill wind blew along the plateau, sending clouds across the sun and raising a flurry of yellow dust.

Something was wrong. Barbier walked quickly toward the prison and stopped. Then he turned and went toward the road as if confused. He turned to the soldiers near the van.

''You! Go to the prison immediately and check on the prisoner. And you! Take the jeep and see if anyone is on the road.''

Barbier paced for several minutes in front of the generals as the Bolivian military men exchanged skeptical glances. The soldier appeared at the door of the prison building and waved his arms. He shouted against the wind and began to run across the camp. The second time he called, Barbier heard the words before they were blown away.

"He's escaped! They're dead! The prisoner has escaped!" Barbier wheeled to face the other soldiers near the van. "Sound the alarm!" he shouted. "Put a line of men across the road. We'll comb the plateau from one end to the other until we find him!"

JESSUP FELL INTO A CROUCH against a building, panting hard, desperately short of breath. The simple application of the pocketknife and matches to the cigar, and some gun powder from a bullet, had produced an effective timing device. He had placed it next to a pile of acetone-soaked rags. But it had taken much too long to do. He had cut his hand trying to pry open a drum of acetone with the pocketknife. It bled badly and hurt like hell. Jessup figured he had anywhere from thirty seconds to a couple of minutes. If it didn't go off by then, he could forget about it.

He began to encircle the camp, moving behind the buildings and coming close to the edge of the plateau. It was a precipice, with a sheer drop to a stone-filled valley hundreds of meters below. The maps had shown the plateau to be the hand at the end of a long, thin arm of rising cliffs. Allowing his eye to follow the natural slant of the plateau, Jessup deduced where the road was. He had covered only about half the distance when he saw the van and jeeps lined up in front of the Institute's administrative building.

The soldiers around the vehicles were talking and joking, not mounting any guard. And they were facing away from him. He took a deep breath, made a wish and scurried across the street to the cover of the next building as fast as his stubby legs could kick dust. His knees sank under him, and he fell to the ground.

Gotta get up, Jessup told himself. He was feeling another onrush of the dreaded vertigo. No time, he mumbled, fighting it, pushing himself to his feet. It wasn't the vertigo. It was the sight of the Bolivian generals marching from the administrative buildings, behind the diminutive, rumpled figure of the man who originally had hired and paid him. Karl Barbier.

For the umpteenth time he asked himself how he could have let himself be dragged into the scheming of an unrepentant Nazi, and for the umpteenth time he heard the same answer—one point six million dollars. So now he was hustling ass across a windswept plateau in the Andes with little chance of getting out alive.

As if to confirm his doubts, a soldier yelled from the building that had housed his cell, and Barbier

reacted angrily. There was only one thing left to do—
hide in the low space underneath the building and
wait for his homemade fuse to burn down. Jessup
got down on his hands and knees and crawled.

He waited.

A quickly organized search party began to search
the camp, building by building. The soldiers worked
their way from the area near the prison. Barbier
shouted orders from the back of jeep, driving back
and forth through the camp raising clouds of yellow
dust.

Jessup prayed for an explosion that refused to
come. It was looking more and more as if his little
improvisation hadn't worked. There wasn't going to
be a diversion.

His only choice was to move from crawl space to
crawl space, making his way slowly across the camp
toward the road. Sooner or later they would flush
him into the open. Maybe, he thought, he should just
make a run for it, try to get to the road and . . .

He stopped himself. He knew it was hopeless. He
said farewell to all the Poire Belle Hélènes he'd ever
loved. Damned if they were going to shoot him up
against the wall. He'd give them a run for their
money. The American way.

He scrambled to the edge of the crawl space, digging his spine painfully into the corner of a beam. He
peered from under the building. It was clear as far as

he could see. He rolled out, jumped to his feet and started running.

He avoided the open quadrant, instead scurrying quickly behind the rows of barracks toward the road. A jeep carrying four soldiers blocked the one way out, and there was still another hundred meters to the dip in the plateau where the road climbed down the side of the mountain. Jessup crept along the wall of the nearest building, the last one in the camp that provided a possibility of cover. Think small, he told himself. Think as small as possible.

The Fixer got his goal firmly in sight, the crest of the gravel road leading off the plateau.

With a last silent prayer, he ran for it.

He was almost a third of the distance across, just at the point where he thought it might be working. They hadn't seen him. He was going to get past them. Hope was making him silly. He was panting hard, and his heart was on the verge of bursting from his overweight body. It was only a matter of milliseconds before—

A rifle shot pinged across the plateau, and earth exploded just behind his heels. He jumped and ran faster, waiting for the next bullet to punch a bloody hole through his heart. Instead, he heard laughing in the distance, and shouts. The jeep's engine roared to life. Another gunshot, and a second bullet exploded at his ankles. A third bullet kicked up clumps of earth and grass, this time in front of him. He swerved, and another bullet pounded past his leg, forcing him to veer aside.

They were playing with him like a cat bouncing a mouse between its paws. The sound of the jeep's engine roared up behind him. He looked over his shoulder long enough to see they were giving chase.

From some unknown source he squeezed last reserves of strength, pouring it into his legs until he ran so fast he didn't think he would be able to stop, even if he wanted to. The sound of his straining heart boomed through his torso and into his head. His lungs kicked in his chest, desperate for more oxygen. Sweat poured down his face and was sucked into his mouth and nose with every desperate breath of air.

Autofire cut a swath across the grass at his heels, sending shudders up his back. The soldiers laughed again. More jeeps, carrying the generals, sped across the quadrant toward the escaping prisoner and joined in the chase.

Karl Barbier's anger ebbed with Jessup's discovery. He couldn't help smiling at the spectacle of the fat man in the dirty white suit trotting across the plateau as fast as his little legs could carry him. He put his feet wide apart to steady himself as he stood in the back of the open jeep. Then he drew his Walther P-38 from his holster, aimed carefully at Jessup's backside and fired.

Jessup yelped as the bullet tore across the left cheek of his rear end. He ran erratically, swerving left and right to confuse his pursuers. The crest at the edge of the plateau was barely twenty meters away, a short horizon of grass and gravel. It was the last thing he asked for from life—to make it that far. He framed his vision around it and drove himself forward. The world beyond the plateau—the mountain peaks jutting into the blue sky, the plump clouds scurrying past, the chill wind hurtling down from the Andes—was suddenly silent. He saw himself running in slow motion. His heart pounded against his rib cage and his lungs ached, yet he no longer felt pain. A sensation of lightness overwhelmed him. His body floated as his legs scrambled madly onto the gravel road. The crest of the plateau was only a few meters away.

The shouts from the jeeps were angry and urgent. More bullets winged their deadly way past him as he darted from side to side, but now they were aiming for keeps. The edge of the plateau was almost within his grasp. Jessup had never seen anything so vividly in his entire life. He stretched out his arms as if he could grab it and pull it to him.

Somehow he knew that if he made it to the edge, he would be free. The thought filled him with a final certainty, and when a jeep suddenly and miraculously rose over the crest of the plateau, it was almost as if he expected it.

The machine gun mounted on the back of the jeep began to blink, and a stream of bullets winged past Jessup's ears into the faces of his pursuers. But nothing prepared him for the great steel bulk of an armored personnel carrier as its engine strained over the final incline.

Jessup stumbled, and his legs collapsed beneath him. The big Texan flew onto his stomach in the dirt as the jeep and the carrier rumbled past. He had one last thought as his face plowed through the gravel. He caught a glimpse of a familiar face. Somehow the SOBs had made it. And so had he.

BEFORE THE SOBs hit the top of plateau, Barrabas heard the sounds of gunfire and the racing engines on the mountain top above them. He turned the wheel of the jeep over to Nate Beck, then scrambled back into the rear to take charge of the British-made L-7 version of the MAG general purpose machine gun. Billy Two fed the disintegrating link belt into the feed mechanism while Barrabas wedged his feet against the base of the tripod and rested his finger firmly against the trigger.

The jeep engine roared and strained against the steep incline that led to the Nazi's mountain redoubt. The sounds of gunfire grew louder. The jeep slowed, its wheels gripping at the gravel road. Suddenly it lurched forward the last few meters, its transmission screaming as it hit the top of the mountain.

The Institute for Linguistic Semantics spread along the flat plateau in front of them. Jeeps from the Bolivian army, filled with high-ranking officers, were careening madly around the wide, flat field between the road and the buildings. Barely five meters in front of him, Walker Jessup chugged down the road. Bullets tore up the ground behind him.

Beck veered sharply aside, barely missing the astonished Fixer. Barrabas squeezed the L-7's hairpin trigger unleashing a withering chain of lead death across the plateau and into the surprised faces of Barbier and company.

The war criminal dropped fearfully as bullets winged dangerously past his head. Bloody flowers bloomed across the chest of the soldier next to him, somersaulting him head over heels off the back of the jeep. "Turn around!" Barbier shouted to the driver.

The driver didn't need to hear it. The sudden arrival of the jeep and the APC rising abruptly over the crest of the road had sown confusion among the merrymaking Nazis. For a moment, the generals and their drivers saw two vehicles of the Bolivian army unexpectedly joining the fun.

The fun was over when the bullets started coming their way. Four jeeps turned en masse and made a beeline back toward the buildings of the Institute.

"Keep after them!" Barrabas yelled at Nate. He pivoted the L-7 to one side and squeezed the trigger, stitching a line of lead along the rear tires of the fleeing vehicles. He raised the barrel and sent another rapid chain of death across the field. The bullets pounded over the heads of the cowering generals, smashing through windshields.

As Karl Barbier and the generals reached the Institute, there was an explosion of bone and blood as the head of one of the drivers disintegrated in the front seat. The jeep flew out of control, smashing violently into the corner of a building. It flipped onto its side, pouring its load of Bolivian generals onto the ground. The panicking officers picked themselves up and hightailed toward the far end of the camp.

Barbier flattened himself against the floor of the jeep as Barrabas's bullets flew overhead like deadly hummingbirds. Something had gone seriously wrong. But the attackers were making a mistake. He grabbed his EM-2 and slipped it to full auto. Crawling carefully on his stomach to the back of the jeep, he slung the barrel over the tailgate and aimed for the white-haired soldier manning the machine gun.

IN THE HUMBER APC, O'Toole pressed the accelerator, slamming into high gear and steadily gaining speed. The Pig roared and quickly matched speed with the jeep as they tore across the flat surface of the Andean plateau.

Lee Hatton stood on the seat between O'Toole and Nanos, pushing open the roof hatch.

"Alex, you feeling any better?" she shouted down, shoving her autorifle ahead of her through the hole.

"Better," the Greek said grimly. Lee had given him Gravol—normally used for sea and air sickness—from her emergency medical kit. The medicine had steadied him out, but his tanned skin was still grayish at the corners of his mouth and around his eyes.

"You still look like death warmed over."

"Thanks for the compliment, babe," the Greek answered morosely. "Let's just call it death." He shifted in his seat and pushed the barrel of his autorifle through the gun port in the door. "Are we seeing any action here, or is the colonel going to do all the work, Liam?"

Through the narrow slit in the Pig's protected windshield, O'Toole saw Barbier open up from the rear of his jeep. "Goddamn," O'Toole cursed. He wound the wheel toward him, trying desperately to cut off Barbier's line of fire.

BARRABAS FELT THE BULLETS PUNCH into his chest as muzzle fire flashed from the tailgate of the fleeing jeep. Agony seared along the side of his body, and warm blood gushed from the torn uniform. The force of the bullets pushed him back from the machine gun.

"You okay?" Billy Two dropped the link belt and reached for him.

"Yeah." Barrabas gritted his teeth and shook his head to clear the stinging pain. "But I think it's going to cost me a couple of ribs."

Nate shouted and ducked under the dashboard, driving blind as another wicked rush of bullets flew across the jeep, peppering the windshield with shatter holes. Barrabas pushed himself up and reached for the machine gun.

Suddenly the Pig careened to the left and drove sideways between the two jeeps.

"Let 'er rip!" the Irishman shouted, swinging from the wheel.

Nanos responded. The twin sounds of autofire from his gun and Lee's reverberated through the APC's cab.

Barbier ducked as the big metal box on wheels drove across the rear of his jeep with its gun ports firing. A bullet skinned his hand, driving his autorifle from his grip. He clenched his teeth against the pain and shouted to the driver.

"Get out! Get out of here!"

The panic-stricken driver steered down the road past the administrative building and over the quadrant. Another jeep was ahead of them, racing for the far end of the camp. Several of the Bolivian generals from the overturned vehicle were running on foot.

The fourth jeep turned in a desperate attempt to circle around the mercs and slip down the road.

"Head him off, Nate!" Barrabas roared. Clenching one hand to his wound to stanch the flow of blood, he grabbed the handle of the L-7 with the other and spun it around. The jeep bucked as Nate floored the accelerator. Barrabas hung on to the machine gun and sent off a stream of hot lead across the front of the escaping vehicle, knocking out its headlights and blowing holes in the rad. A spray of water and steam blew from the hood. The generals cowered below the seats as the driver turned madly and headed back through the buildings of the Institute.

Barbier, the generals and the last of the elite soldiers trained as the Fiancés of Death had retreated to the far end of the camp. They prepared their last stand, circling the three remaining jeeps in a line in front of a corrugated metal building. Soldiers rushed outside carrying weapons and ammunition and took up position behind the protective wall of army vehicles.

Suddenly the mercs encountered a wall of serious enemy fire.

"Pull it over!" Barrabas shouted to Nate.

Attacking in the open jeep amounted to little more than a suicide run against the entrenched Nazis. Beck braked, pulling into the protection of one of the buildings near the quadrant. O'Toole pulled in parallel to them with the door of the Pig swinging open.

"Get in back and use the gun ports!" the Irishman yelled. "We'll make a pass right in front of their noses."

Barrabas, Beck and Billy Two grabbed their autorifles and hopped from the jeep.

Suddenly there was a blood-curdling shout of total panic from enemy lines at the far end of the plateau. The scream was cut abruptly by the deafening roar of an awesome explosion as the buildings at the far end of the Institute blew into a wall of flame.

WALKER JESSUP LAY FACEDOWN in the gravel listening to the machine gun fire. Slowly his breath returned to him, and with it a small part of his energy. He pushed himself up and flipped over. Barrabas's arrival was the kind of miracle he could almost predict—if only in retrospect. But the improvised fuse that had failed to ignite the acetone-soaked rags still nagged at him.

In answer, the Andean plateau trembled slightly, and the buildings of the Institute quivered. Suddenly an ear-shattering explosion washed across the thin mountain air. Balls of liquid flame floated over the end of the plateau, imploding and dropping like a curtain of fire across the Institute. More explosions rippled through the chemical storage yard, belching bubbles of fire into the Bolivian sky. Ether and acetone fell in a rain of liquid fire, splashing down on the roofs of the buildings, on the grassy quadrant and on the heads and backs of Barbier and his cocaine generals.

Waves of fire spread almost instantly among the Institute's wooden buildings. A chorus of mind-numbing screams rose from the plateau as the Bolivian soldiers were transformed into human torches. Some rolled on the ground in a futile effort to smother the napalmlike fire that clung to their flesh. Others panicked as the flames licked through their clothing. They tried to run. There was nowhere to go. They fell from the sheer precipices at the edge of the plateau like errant spinning balls of Saint Elmo's fire.

Protected by the wall of the building, the mercs felt the wind of the firestorm sweep past, carrying with it a death-dealing maelstrom of heat and metal debris.

"Get in back!" Barrabas ordered Beck, shouting over the roar of the fiery hurricane. The merc ran for the back of the Pig. Hatton leaped from the cab and ran to Barrabas's side as O'Toole reversed the heavy carrier and turned it back toward the road.

"Where in hell's Billy Two?" she yelled, looking around the jeep. The Osage had disappeared.

"Doesn't matter," Barrabas told her. The Indian warrior bought his own time. And paid for it, if he

had to. "Let's get out of here before we're barbe-
cued."

BILLY TWO STOOD IN THE MIDST of the burning
buildings as the searing waves of heat washed over
him. He tore off the tight-fitting Bolivian army shirt
and ripped the pants into a crudely fashioned loin-
cloth.

The heat didn't bother him. He was an Osage
warrior again. Hawk Spirit had told him that something was to be found in the eye of the fire. He was
to wait there for it. Soon he saw what it was.

A short, older man with a paunch was furtively
making his way among the burning buildings. Karl
Barbier ran with his head up, watching the heaven for
swatches of burning liquid falling from the explod-
ing drums of acetone. His clothes were torn and in
some places burned from his body.

You're looking at a million bucks, Billy Two heard
someone say.

Barbier made his way across the quadrant in the
direction of von Rausch's van. The mobile gas
chamber was still parked in front of the burning administrative building. He was exhausted, his mind
numb as he watched his world transformed into a
flaming conflagration that roared in his ears. Pain
screamed up and down the right side of his body. He
had been badly burned. The skin split and oozed. He
could barely walk, but he knew there was safety be-

yond the flames—in the capital city of La Paz. Von Rausch's van was his last chance.

He fell against the hood, screamed and jumped back. The metal was burning hot. He opened the door and reached up to climb behind the wheel when a hand took him by the collar and lifted him off the ground.

"No," a deep, solemn voice proclaimed. "I drive. You ride back here." Billy Two carried the man, who kicked feebly, to the back of the van.

"No! No! Not in there! Please, not in there," Barbier begged.

"Hmph." Billy Two threw him inside the stainless-steel compartment, slammed the doors and locked him in. He climbed into the cab. The seat was so hot it burned his skin. That was Hawk Spirit's style. He faded in and out in his own good time. Suddenly he was gone, and Billy Two zapped back to reality. He was half naked at the wheel of a four-by-four van with hellfire burning all around him. The vehicle was sizzling hot, and the gas tank was liable to go off any second.

He turned over the engine, slipping it into gear. The van lurched forward a few inches, responding with infinite slowness to the desperate pressures of his foot on the gas pedal. There was only one thing to do. Trust in Hawk Spirit. And drive like hell.

THE MERCS STOOD NEAR THE ROAD at the edge of the plateau, watching the Institute burn. Lee Hatton leaned over Walker Jessup, listening to his heartbeat with a stethoscope.

"You know Barbier's worth a million bucks, too!" the Fixer complained. "And we missed it. He's in there somewhere burned to a crisp."

"That's why it's so hard for me to believe you got taken in by it, Walker."

Jessup dug a handful of dirt from the ground and threw it away. "I'm sure glad my message got through to you. On their own, the generals who seized power won't last long. But with these vipers feeding off them, Bolivia might have become the cornerstone of a new Reich. But how did you know about the Institute?"

"The bank, Walker."

"The bank?"

"We broke into your safety deposit box at the bank."

"Oh." The Fixer nodded and looked thoughtful.

Lee stood up and put her stethoscope away. "It's practically normal, Walker. Almost athletic."

"Looks like this little adventure did you some good, Jessup," Barrabas said, smiling.

"But not you," Hatton told him. "Let me have a look at those ribs now and that hole in your side."

"The morphine has steadied me, Lee. The rest will wait. Look! Our ride out of here's arriving." He stared into the sky, past the snowy peak of Illimani. A helicopter was clearly visible. The distant sound of its rotors grew steadily through the thunderous roar of the fire.

The smile on Lee's face came from something more than just the prospect of going home.

"Ahem." Walker Jessup cleared his throat as he stood. He sauntered over to Barrabas and spoke quietly. "You didn't happen to find anything else in the safety deposit box, did you?"

Barrabas thought for a moment. He shook his head. "Nope. Can't say we did."

Jessup nodded again, considering how to approach the subject of his money.

"Colonel, looks like Billy Two's on his way back," Nanos called.

Barrabas turned toward the Institute. A van appeared between the flame-licked frames of the wooden buildings. It gained speed, rapidly emerging from the ring of fire. The ancient vehicle lumbered down the road, with Billy Two waving from the cab. He stopped in front of the waiting mercs and climbed out.

"I have brought you your million-dollar man. He rides there." Billy jerked his thumb toward the rear with a proud smile.

"Really?" Jessup said, his eyes lighting up. "You have him? Perhaps not all is lost." He scurried toward the van. The mercs followed. Billy Two opened the door. Karl Barbier leered stiffly at attention, his eyes bulging furiously and his tongue protruding obscenely. He stood perfectly still for a moment, then leaned slowly forward, tumbling onto the ground where he broke into a crumpled heap.

The mercs looked puzzled. Billy Two grabbed Barbier by his shoulder and shook him. He was clearly dead.

"Get back," Barrabas said, retreating from the van.

"Carbon monoxide," Lee said. "The back of the van must be full of it."

"Von Rausch was the inventor of the mobile gas chamber, wasn't he?" Barrabas asked the Fixer.

Jessup swallowed slowly. He realized he was looking at the fate that had been intended for him.

"Colonel?" Nate Beck approached, carrying the cardboard document case. "We still have this!" He dangled it in front of the Fixer.

"My fee!" Jessup grabbed for it, but came up empty. Barrabas snatched it away before he got there.

He turned it over and dumped the wads of currency onto the grass.

"My fee," Jessup said again weakly.

"Fee hell. I'll send you the bill for medical and out-of-pocket expenses, Jessup. As for this one point six million dollars—" Barrabas picked up two bundles and tossed them to Nate "—that makes two for you. And two for Alex, two for Lee, two for Billy."

Jessup stifled a sputter of indignation as Barrabas threw the money to his mercs. His hand kept darting forward in hopeful anticipation of hearing his own name.

"Two for O'Toole, two for me." Barrabas stuffed the money inside his shirt and put the rest back in the document case. "And two each for Geoff Bishop and Claude Hayes."

The helicopter was closing in on the plateau. It skated back and forth in greeting.

Nile Barrabas smiled magnanimously at Jessup and winked. "We share everything. The blood, the battles and the money."

His imprisonment and escape from almost certain death had strained the Fixer's emotions to their limit. Seeing his money disappear into the hands of the SOBs pushed him over the edge. His face crumpled, and tears came to his eyes.

Barrabas slapped the Texan on the back and hung his arm loosely around the fat man's neck as the helicopter came in for a landing. "That's why they call us mercenaries."

**Nile Barrabas and the
Soldiers of Barrabas are the**

by Jack Hild

Nile Barrabas is a nervy son of a bitch who
was the last American soldier out of Vietnam
and the first man into a new kind of action. His
warriors, called the Soldiers of Barrabas, have
one very simple ambition: to do what the
Marines can't or won't do. Join the Barrabas
blitz! Each book hits new heights—this is
brawling at its best!

"Nile Barrabas is one tough SOB himself. . . .
A wealth of detail. . . . SOBs does the job!"
—*West Coast Review of Books*

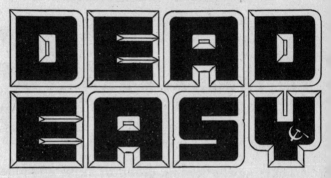

TAKE 'EM NOW

FOLDING SUNGLASSES
FROM GOLD EAGLE

Mean up your act with these tough, street-smart shades. Practical, too, because they fold 3 times into a handy, zip-up polyurethane pouch that fits neatly into your pocket. Rugged metal frame. Scratch-resistant acrylic lenses. Best of all, they can be yours for only $6.99. **MAIL ORDER TODAY.**

Send your name, address, and zip code, along with a check or money order for just $6.99 + .75¢ for postage and handling (for a total of $7.74) payable to Gold Eagle Reader Service, a division of Worldwide Library. New York and Arizona residents please add applicable sales tax.

Remove from pouch...

unfold once...

unfold twice...

and they're ready to wear.

Gold Eagle Reader Service
901 Fuhrmann Blvd.
P.O. Box 1325
Buffalo, N.Y. 14240-1325

GOLD EAGLE

GES1–RRR

Offer not available in Canada.

4 FREE BOOKS
1 FREE GIFT
NO RISK
NO OBLIGATION
NO KIDDING

SPECIAL LIMITED-TIME OFFER

Mail to **Gold Eagle Reader Service**

In the U.S.
901 Fuhrmann Blvd.
P.O. Box 1394
Buffalo, N.Y. 14240-1394

In Canada
P.O. Box 609
Fort Erie, Ont.
L2A 9Z9

YEAH! Rush me 4 free Gold Eagle novels and my free mystery bonus. Then send me 6 brand-new novels every other month as they come off the presses. Bill me at the low price of just $14.95— a 13% saving off the retail price. There are no shipping, handling or other hidden costs. There is no minimum number of books I must buy. I can always return a shipment and cancel at any time. Even if I never buy another book from Gold Eagle, the 4 free novels and the mystery bonus are mine to keep forever.

Name   (PLEASE PRINT)

Address   Apt. No.

City   State/Prov.   Zip/Postal Code

Signature (If under 18, parent or guardian must sign)

This offer is limited to one order per household and not valid to present subscribers. Price is subject to change.

166-BPM-BP6F